TRUST ME 3

KÄIXO

KÄIXO BOOKS PUBLISHING

ALSO BY KÄIXO

Promising My Love to a Boss Series:

Promising My Love to a Boss

Promising My Love to a Boss 2

Promising My Love to a Boss 3

Promising My Love to a Boss 4

Bankroll Boyz Series:

Give Me All of You

Give Me All of You 2

Give Me All of You 3

Carter & Amani [Continuing Series]:

Trust Me

Trust Me 2

Standalone Books:

Rein

And so much more to come!

For finding true love...

If there's a book that you want to read, but it hasn't been written yet, then you must write it.

TONI MORRISON

CONTENTS

CHAPTER ONE

Amani

Pecking the keys on my laptop, one-by-one, I groaned for the fourth time and rolled my eyes as it went unnoticed by my babbling little sisters. *Who could blame them, though?* I was never on their radar. Usually a wallflower, my sudden stroke of luck wouldn't change that. Pausing in between taps, my lips twisted as *Dreams* by *Fleetwood Mac* caught my attention. It wasn't unusual for me to play music in the background, especially love sappy songs... I'm a cancer and we're broody, emotional, and highly nostalgic—Still, the chorus resonated with my spirit.

Thunder only happens when it's raining
Players only love you when they're playing

Nibbling on my bottom lip, these words were the furthest things from the truth, concerning my relationship... But they were sad and that's exactly how I've been feeling for a while. Since having Dot and graduating, my reality was finally settling in. And it didn't look like blue skies and sunshines for the rest of my natural-born life. I was thousands of miles from home and I couldn't do it. Any of this. Being a wife and a mother seemed like a piece of cake but I know me. Everything in my life, since birth had been chaotic. From the way my parents conceived me even until the day Jewel pushed me through the side of the living... She had sowed discord and disenchantment for most of her life, leaving the reaping of her sins for the three souls she birthed and left behind in this world. I guess that's why I was back in school, again, trying to keep my mind from circling the drain.

I mean, I was already becoming Jewel because I couldn't take care of my daughter. Well, not without Carter. He had to physically be in the nursery with me or else Chandler Banks would have a fit. It's like, I knew I loved her but there was no emotional connection. I didn't even jump into action, hearing her cries from the baby monitor. Of course, I'd do my best to calm her down... But most of the time, I wasn't enough.

"*Bitch—Who* is that?" Salimah's voice popped into my head as I quickly came back to the phone call I was supposed to be having.

"*Who* is *what*?" Fatima was lost, as usual.

"The music—*Mani?*" She knew it was me, yet she had to ask.

"Yeah?" I still answered back.

"Why you listening to that?"

"Because I'm writing my paper," I quipped.

"You okay?" Salimah asked, but I knew her question was a trap.

If I told my sisters how melancholy I'd been, Salimah would be the first to berate me. In her mind, I had it all: the man, the life, and the kids. And I did. Carter was everything I never dreamed of having. Single-handedly, this man had come into my life and performed the miracle Cinderella's fairy godmother could only bestow upon her for a few hours of the night... I'd gotten the dress, the up-do, the carriage, the prince, and the iconic glass slippers—But I was still unhappy.

Misery, thy name is Amani. *Ugh!* Why am I so mopey? I have everything I could ever want and if I don't... Carter will make it happen. And trust me, I've tested the realms of his generosity to no end—In his own words, *"Whateva you want mama—I gotchu!"* And, yes, my husband is a man of his word. So, why can't I be normal and appreciative? Because I don't deserve this. Any of it.

From the spacious mansion we live in to the four acres it's built on. This life is mine but it shouldn't be. I don't want it anymore. I can't take it. I shouldn't. I'm a city girl—No, not as in, *Real ass bitch give a fuck about a nigga...* No! But I'm a Chicagoan and I've always been in the city. Born and bred. That's all I know, and it's where I want to be—*No, scratch that...* It's where I *need* to be.

"Why you so quiet?" Salimah went with another approach because she knew if she offended me too much, I'd withdraw from this conversation completely.

"I'm just letting y'all talk," I sighed, this time hearing Salimah growl because she knew there was an underlined meaning behind my sound effects.

"Bitch, *what* is it?" Always crass, I didn't expect a red carpet ride with this particular little sister. *"Tsk! Oh!"* Salimah giggled as my ears perked, knowing whatever came out of her mouth next wouldn't be why I was moping. "We ain't even ask how yo first Mother's Day was—I saw the post from Carter... He is so sweet!" Salimah cooed as Fatima chimed in. "He does not come off as the romantic type, girl—I'm impressed!" Salimah went on as I rolled my eyes to the side.

"He was romantic for the baby shower!" Fatima interjected.

"Not like this—I mean, he played his part... Making the evening about his woman, which every man should," Salimah went down a list of things she assumed every man should do. "But he was like one of the guys. How Ty and Torin always is—"

"No..." I had to cut Salimah off. "He's nothing like Torin."

"*Tsk!* Don't do my baby!" Fatima was now offended. "Yes, he has his days when he's a grouch but he's all about me," Fatima's voice reeked of confidence in her words and me and Salimah could attest to that. "And I got that man wrapped around *all ten* fingers and toes—"

"*Damn, bitch*—Tell *us* how you really feel, then!" Salimah cackled as me and Fatima joined her.

Torin was definitely all for my baby sister. You couldn't breathe wrong near her and not have him down your throat about it. Whether right or wrong, *Joseph* was going to go to bat for *Fatty Ma. Dats on da gang!* And the more I sat here thinking over my sister's words, the more I realized how much Carter and Torin had in common. Maybe not as aggressive with my sisters but he let nobody come at me sideways. Granted, he didn't have a valid reason to mistreat my sisters like Torin did with us... But you know what I mean.

"I'm just saying..." Fatima cleared her throat, and I prepared for her to clear up her words. "I know how he comes off to y'all and there're times when I'm tapping him, trying to reel him back in—But he only does that because he knows..." Fatima's words trailed off and suddenly I felt awkward. "You know? And I won't lie like I don't like it because I love and appreciate him for it—In some ways it's those moments that give me the strength to come out of my shell," Fatima admitted and in this moment I envied her being able to live in her truth as I wallowed in unnecessary self-pity. "Because I know... Without a shadow of a doubt—My man will air *dis* bitch out!" Fatima had me and Salimah laughing.

"Don't we know it," I agreed with Fatima as I giggled.

"And I believe Ty would do the same—"

"Without question!" Salimah couldn't wait to speak on her husband.

"I mean, he's a Taylor—It's embedded in their DNA," I mumbled to myself.

"And after that phone stunt Carter pulled—"

"Girl!" Salimah chimed in, cutting off Fatima.

"He has some *Joseph tendencies,*" Fatima finished as I smirked and nodded.

"*Girl*—And Ty told me how yo ass snuck over BJ's crib—"

"What?" Fatima cut Salimah off as I exhaled from embarrassment.

"Yes!" Salimah was on a roll. "Why you think he was changing her number in the first place?" Salimah had shut me out the conversation as she and our baby sister went back and forth.

"You went to go see BJ after you and Carter got together?" Fatima asked as I pursed my lips together, hating they were rehashing old news.

"No," I rolled my eyes as Salimah cackled.

"Don't lie, bitch—"

"I'm not—It's not like how y'all are making it out to be," I was trying to find the words to clarify. "Brandon sent me this long text about how he was leaving the city for good and he wanted to see me—"

"So yo goofy ass trotted over to his crib to do what?" Salimah grilled me as my shoulders fell in frustration.

I wanted to be mad at my little sister but I couldn't. She was right. Hearing my actions repeated to me didn't exactly sound like I'd made the correct decision. There was nothing between me and BJ, so why did I go? I can't even recall what was going through my head during that time, either. Was I having second thoughts about Carter? Did I think there was something to rekindle between me and Brandon? No, of course not!

"*Hello*?"

"I'm here—Guys, I don't wanna talk about this," I groaned hearing Salimah snicker.

"Figures—"

"So, did y'all do anything?" Fatima must've had too much wax in her ears because she wasn't listening to me.

"No!" My defenses were up. "Why would you ask me that?"

I neglected to tell them about the kiss because I didn't need another round of third degree. Especially not while Salimah was on the phone. Fatima would be more understanding and not as quick to judge me. Although, her tone would reflect how she truly felt... She had enough empathy to keep her comments to herself.

"He came to my house—"

"What?" Salimah and I both gasped in disbelief.

"Yeah," Fatima giggled to herself. "He startled me and almost got his ass beat by Torin," she laughed a little more as I smirked, remembering the beat down Carter had given him. "He was looking for you."

"Of course he was," Salimah grumbled. "That's all he be doing these days."

"No, he doesn't," I couldn't catch the words before they slipped out of my mouth.

"*Uh*," Salimah croaked. "And how you know?" Salimah questioned me. "Cuz I know y'all ain't still talkin' and textin'!" She was doing the most.

"No, I'm just saying..." I sighed. "I'm not the only thing on his mind—Brandon is a narcissistic, gaslighting, asshole," I growled, hearing Fatima breathe heavily as Salimah giggle.

"*Oou!*" Salimah added to her laughter. "I'm tellin'!" She sang as me and Fatima laughed with her.

"Shut up," I couldn't stop smiling. "I just don't need y'all thinking I have feelings for that nigga—"

"Okay, *then*, tell us how you really feel!" Salimah probably couldn't take hearing me cursing or just speaking like she'd normally speak, but I was sick of this conversation.

"No, I'm cool," I lied.

"No, you're not," Fatima caught it. "What's wrong, *Boobie*?"

I hadn't heard that name in years. Swallowing my spit, there was a faint salty taste in the back of my throat and I knew what would follow if I didn't get myself together. It's been months since I thought about Jewel and I wasn't gonna start back up. Since her murder, I'd convinced myself that her leaving earth was best for me. She never truly fulfilled her role as my mother and things weren't going to change either. Still, I couldn't understand why one nickname was tugging on my tear ducts so heavily. I hadn't felt this emotional since I sat adjacent from my father in the booth at the Original Pancake House. And that was only because I was overwhelmed. He was a stranger to me with all these unheard stories of who Jewel was and I guess... I just had a momentary lapse in character or whatever but I've managed to keep my feelings under wrap.

"You think I should come up for a visit?" I sniffled as I wiped the corner of my left eye.

"*Huh*?" Fatima felt the dodge, but it still caught her off guard.

"I miss you guys," I tried to play it off.

"Yo ass don't miss us!" Salimah clicked as my bottom lip quivered. "*Bitch*, what's goin' on?" she asked.

"I think I made a mistake!" I burst into tears. "I'm not supposed to be here—I don't have anybody," I sobbed, covering my face even though I was the only person here. "I was thriving back home," my shoulders dropped as I thought about my bartending job and cashier get up I had with Walgreens. "I could've just finished school and—"

"And what?" Salimah interjected. "Chase behind Brandon goofy ass? Amani, what's really goin' on? Is Carter mistreating you?"

"No!" I was quick to dub those thoughts.

"So, what?" she was sounding like the big sister. "Where is he?"

"He went to pick up Ro—"

"Where's Dot?" Salimah was running the show with all these questions.

"With him—"

"What—*Why*?"

Clenching my jaw tightly, I didn't want to admit to my little sisters that Carter was the better parent. Especially when I've watched how they interacted with their children. It was effortless to them. Even with all three of us having Jewel as an example... My little sisters switched gears and made sure my nieces and nephews knew they were loved and cared for. Not to say I didn't love Chandler because I did... There was just something missing. I don't even remember how I felt when she came into this world and Dot was only four months. I want to say I was happy, but that day is a blur.

"Mani, I can't say, for sure, how things are going now but I saw you and Carter at your baby shower," Fatima started and I didn't need her to finish to know where she was going with it. "And you definitely didn't look like that here—"

"You were barely around me!" I snapped, knowing I misplaced my anger with my sisters because I couldn't accept my reality.

Silence ensued and had me regretting my words or the way I said them. Inhaling quietly, this wasn't what I wanted. Not right now. I was used to bottling up my emotions and going on about my business... But lately, it's been hard to get past anything without my mind replaying my biggest fault. I was great with Cairo, or so I thought. I mean, I could cook most of his favorite foods and order the rest—It's just for my own child. I was circling the drain, and I knew once I failed with Chandler, I'd be no different from Jewel.

"Do you need us to come down there?" Fatima softly spoke up instead of copping an attitude.

"Fuck asking—We comin'!" Salimah chimed in as I clenched my jaw, looking off to the side where the door was to see Carter leaning against the frame.

Startled, I gasped, dropping my phone from my ear. Hearing it crash against my laptop. Judging from the look on his face, I know he heard a lot of our conversation. Picking my phone up while tucking my bottom lip into my mouth, I couldn't do anything but end the conversation.

"Hey—I'm gonna call y'all later."

Not waiting for goodbye, I pressed the red phone button and lowered my iPhone. Lifting my laptop from my lap so I could move it to the side, Carter was already making his way into our bedroom. He kept his eyes on me until he hit the corner and disappeared. Tucking my bottom lip into my mouth, my phone chirped from the incoming messages. Probably my sisters letting me know they didn't appreciate being hung up on. Dropping my shoulders, I was tempted to pick my phone up and read them when Carter came back into the bedroom, still looking at me.

"Hey."

My greeting didn't sound genuine and I could tell by the scowl on his face he'd picked up on it. Still, I was backed up against the wall, so there was no turning back now.

"How was she?"

Clenching his jaw as he got closer to the bed, his eyes were piercing my soul right now, and I wanted to crawl into my shell and never resurface. The only thoughts running through my mind was how much he'd heard and if I could talk my way out of it.

"Can you like talk to me?" I blurted out, feeling like I would melt if he kept this death stare up.

"Are you gon' *like* tell da truth?" On top of mimicking me, his question was confusing, and it was written all over my face, too. "Then I ain't got shit to say—"

"Carter, what—" regaining some composure, I took a deep breath, reaching for his hand before he could turn away from me. "*Wait*—Why are you acting like this?"

"Don't do dat shit, Amani," Carter quickly snatched his hand from mine forcing me to jump out of bed to get in front of him.

"Do what?" I chuckled like I was clueless but I knew what he meant.

Grabbing my arms forcefully, Carter shook me a little, squeezing both arms as he inhaled. Flexing his jawline as he gazed into my eyes, I could hear him telling me to stop playing with him even with his mouth clenched shut. Releasing me just as Dot began to cry, I dropped my shoulders in defeat.

"We gon' knuckle up," Carter mumbled as he flicked my chin before leaving me standing in the middle of the bedroom.

Crossing my arms over my chest, Dot's wailing seemed to get louder until I could hear Carter gently shushing her. *I just want to be able to have that effect her.* Once in my life... *God, I just need that!*

CHAPTER TWO

Carter

Uh, I bet I shake the room
Ayy, Woo, woo, woo
Swerve
Skrrt, skrrt, skrrt

Rolling through Dede's complex my eyes fell on the boys running up and down the court. Spotting Cairo, almost immediately, I smirked while watching my son glide and shine as he showcased his skills. Being a true South Dallas nigga, football was my passion, and I excelled in it from pop warner all the way up to high school graduation. I had scholarships and scouts hounding me but I knew who I was destined to be. And it wasn't suited up for game day on ESPN. But Cairo was different—And I realized that from the moment I first held him. He wasn't like me or my Pops and I wouldn't force him into my lifestyle... Despite how much he looked like me and tried his hardest to emulate me. If I did nothing else in life, I'd make sure all my kids grew up to be better than me and our family. Even in all its splendor the streets loved no one and although fair... This game was cold.

BEEP! BEEP!

Cairo fumbled the ball in his hands as his head shot up to see who was blowing at them. Grinning from ear-to-ear, I watched him shake up with his niggas while slyly slipping his arm around the waist of a little girl who'd popped up out of nowhere. Chuckling and shaking my head, I couldn't deny how much Cairo had inherited from me. Always been a ladies' man and marriage didn't stop that. *Shit, just look at Dot... That lil girl lives in my arms.*

"Wussup, Daddy!" Cairo hopped in front, holding his palm up like I was one of his boys.

Grinning as I slid my palm across his, the smirk on my son's face grew wider. Tossing his bag in the back, I paused, giving him a slight stare down until he realized what I was waiting on.

"Aw, my bad!" Cairo reached to his right for the seatbelt and clicked it on. "Where Dot and Mani?"

"Mani at home—Dot wit, Meemaw," I told him as I swerved off. "Yo mama home?"

"Yeah, my auntie too," Cairo immediately killed any interest to pop into Dede crib by mentioning Dedra.

I'll just text shawty, I thought to myself as we drove out of the complex. Turning the music down, it was time to find out how Cairo was doing this week. School was out, and he was spending a lot of time outside plus, I wanted to know who the little girl was he was hugging on before he got in my truck.

"How you been?"

"*Ah*, you know... Same ole—Different day," Cairo yawned causing me to smirk. "I been ballin' doe—And guess what?" His eyes suddenly lit up as his voice raised an octave. "Playstation five coming out!"

Sucking my teeth before chuckling, that was the last thing I expected to hear out of his mouth but I should've expected it. All this boy does, besides ball is play that damn game. From Fortnite to Call of Duty... He stayed holed up inside his room with the headset, yelling orders and skipping showers.

"You think you finna get dat?" I laughed like he wasn't spoiled as Cairo arrogantly scoffed.

"Somebody gon' get it for me!" Cairo waggled his brows making me laugh even harder. "I'ma tell Mani to get it!"

"I'ma tell her not to—"

"She not gon' listen to you!" Cairo retorted as I eyed him from the side.

"How you figure dat?"

"Cuz she love me—"

"She love me more," I countered, smugly.

"Right, so since she love you and you my daddy she gon' cop dat!" Cairo's logic was flawed but his confidence kept me laughing.

"I'm her daddy so she ain't goin'—"

"*Ugh!*" Cairo's face curled up in disgust as I busted up laughing. "*Tsk!* I'ma tell her you said dat," Cairo smacked his lips as I shrugged, still laughing at his reaction. "Where we bouta eat at?" he sang as my shoulders rose and fell again.

"Where you wanna go?"

"Y'all ain't cook?" Cairo had the nerve to ask as I shook my head.

I didn't know if Amani got off her laptop since I left this morning, but I doubt it. She had a big term paper coming up, and I didn't stress her with house shit when the semesters were ending. School was important to her, and I valued how much she stuck to her goal of becoming an international interpreter.

"Maybe tomorrow—You want Chinese?" I asked Cairo as he shook his head.

"You know mama Chinese us to death," he groaned as I grinned. "I'm tired of general tso. Meemaw probably cooked something," he suggested with his index finger lifted in the air. "We'll see when we get Dot."

"Boy you a trip," I chuckled as I turned into Lake Ridge Estates. "Who was Shawty at da court?" I finally asked as Cairo chuckled nervously. "Nah, who dat is?" I teased, causing his cheeks to burn red.

"She be there all da time," he told me and I knew he was feeling her.

"Dat ain't what I asked you—"

"Her name, Ma'Kirah," he quickly admitted as my smiling continued to make him uncomfortable. "Don't tell mama about dis," Cairo begged only making his current situation more humorous. "*Tsk!* Man—"

"I ain't gon' tell her—Chill out," I promised him just as I reached my parents' house.

"And don't mention it to Meemaw either!" he quickly warned as I shook my head. "She worse than my mama," he mumbled while opening up his door.

"My mama ain't gon' trip—"

"Maybe not wit you and uncle Lin but I'm her only grandson," Cairo stuck out his chest like his words made him superior to me and my brother.

Nigga please, I'm Megan's favorite, I thought as we skipped up the steps to the front door. Using my key, I let us in to Dot screaming at the top of her lungs. *Daddy's here, baby!* Rushing after the sound of her cries, I found my mama and Dot in the kitchen.

"She's getting her teeth," my mama told me as she motioned for me to keep my daughter from toppling over in her bouncer as she turned her back to open the freezer. "I made jello balls earlier and partially froze em so she can chew on em," she told me as my face curled in confusion.

"She too young—"

"She's on solids now and I made sure they're small enough so she won't choke—I used to do it for you and your brother, *Bubba,*" Megan always enjoyed reminding me how she raised me and Collin before I even had kids. "Besides, this recipe is just gonna melt in her mouth after a couple minutes of back and forth... I just want to get her gums cold enough to numb the pain," she told me as I nodded my head up and down.

Stepping back as I watched my mama place one ball into Dot's mouth, quickly shutting down her tantrum of tears.

"Mmm," she hummed causing me and my mama to laugh.

"*See,* Meemaw knows all the tricks, Dotty," my mama kissed her soft forehead as she continued sucking and cooing. "Give her two more after this one dissolves and she should be okay for a few hours," my mama instructed. "I'll be right back."

"Where you goin'?" I asked before she could fully excuse herself.

"To see my grandson—"

"Tsk, say, man..." I groaned, causing my mama to giggle. "Dis why he think he can get whatever he want," I pointed at her as she shrugged.

"As my baby should!" My mama stated nonchalantly. "What is it that he wants?"

"A PlayStation five—"

"I'll get it," she quickly offered, like I knew she would.

"Nah," I shook my head while lifting Dot from her bouncer. "You gon' stop gettin' him everything he ask for," I reprimanded my mama playfully as she coyly shoved me before walking out of the kitchen. "Ya brother gettin' outta hand," I told Dot as she whimpered a little. "*Eh,* cut dat out!" I lightly scolded as her bottom lip quivered. "You, me and Ro gon' have a conversation later on today," I said while grabbing another jello ball and placing it inside Dot's mouth.

Slob running from her mouth down her chin, I knew Dot was completely satisfied. Kissing the side of her face, she gripped my shirt, and I left the kitchen to find my dad. In the den talking back to the TV, I smirked and knocked lightly against the wall to catch his attention.

"Hey!" his face lit up when he noticed Dot in my arms. "Hey pretty girl!" he reached for her and I obliged by handing her over. "What's all this drippin' down your face?" he questioned my baby girl as she sucked on the jello while squealing happily. "I see Meemaw set ya straight," he used the damp folded napkin he placed underneath beer as a makeshift coaster to dry her chin a little.

"*Eeyouuu!*" Dot grinned as my dad's smiled brightened.

"Yeah!" he cheered her on before turning his attention to me. "How's Mani doing?"

"A lot better now dat dis semester is endin'," I told him as he nodded, reaching for the remote to turn down the volume on the TV.

Although I didn't lie, I wasn't telling the complete truth. Yes, Amani wasn't entirely frazzled, but she wasn't as happy as I'd seen her. Something was off between us and no matter how well she thought she hid it from me, those frequent phone calls home, to her sisters, let me know they had something to do with her sullen state.

"I thought classes stopped after may," my dad said as he readjusted Dot in his lap, turning her to the side and laying her head back as she fought what was inevitably coming next. "No, no, no—Nap time," he spoke softly to her as the rocking followed soon after.

"They do, normally but you can choose to take summer classes to speed things along," I told my father as his left brow furrowed.

"So, what—She'll finish by winter?" he caught on quickly as I nodded my head. "Why so soon?"

Raising my shoulders, I really didn't have an answer. Yeah, we all knew what Amani was going to school to become, but she already has the bachelors to do it. I think school had become her distraction and my father's question actually put a few things in perspective for me. I needed to find out what was ailing her. Or lift her spirits, in general. I'd taken notice of how she interacts with everybody in our house, especially Dot. She got along better with Cairo and yeah, that's great and all but my son was usually easygoing. Not that Dot was trouble from the getgo... I just know some mothers need a little extra help to assume their role to their children.

"Carter," my dad tapped me, bringing me out of my head.

"*Huh?*"

"You alright?" he asked me as I nodded my head. "You sure?" he checked again as my eyes shifted down to see Dot soundly sleeping.

"Yeah, I'm good," I told him again, this time pulling my phone from my pocket to check the time and if Amani had called or texted me.

My phone wasn't on silent and if it rang, vibrate was also

turned on too. Running my tongue over my lips, I knew it was time to cut my visit short.

"I gotta go," I told my father as I shot up from the chair next to the sofa. "I know Ro hungry and Mani prolly is too," I talked as I lifted Dot from his arms.

Careful not to wake her, I placed her head against my shoulder, patting her back as she jolted in her sleep. Dot was notorious for cat naps and I wanted to break her from it. We took full naps in this family... No surprises!

"I'll hit y'all back in a couple days," I smirked as my father chuckled, reaching for his sweating bottle of beer.

"You'll be back tomorrow," he grinned before taking a swig.

"Yeah, prolly," I laughed, dapping his knuckle after he sat his drink down.

"Get that girl out them books and treat her to something nice!" My father called out to me as I left the den.

"I'm already on it!" I yelled back, wishing I hadn't because Dot's head shot up so fast, I cursed shortly after. "C'mon, Shawty, close them eyes," I tried forcing her head down, but she wasn't going. *"Tsk! Man!"* I breathed heavily just as Cairo came down the steps. "Perfect timin' Ro, c'mon," I motioned for him to head to the door. "Where my mama at?"

"Right here—What's goin' on?" My mama came around the corner with a to-go plate. "He don't need dat," I told her as I watched Cairo reach for the plate, anyway. "We finna go pick up some food."

"You still can," my mama told me before kissing the top of Cairo's head. "My baby can eat—"

"Yeah, I can," I cut her off, knowing she wasn't talking about me.

"Hush!" My mama laughed as Cairo nudged my side. "You know who I was talking about—And you too, chunky girl!" My mama pinched Dot's thigh as the corners of my baby girl's mouth curled into a smile. "Don't forget the jello, *Bubba*," she reminded me because I sholl forgot. "And I'll see my babies tomorrow!" My mama stepped back to pull Cairo into her arms for one more kiss.

"You sound like yo husband, in there," I told my mama as she giggled.

"That's cuz you can't stay away from here if we paid you— And I'm tempted to shell out a couple dollars for some alone time with my wife," my dad came out his den to put his two cents in.

"*Tsk,* cut it out," I could feel my face tighten with embarrassment knowing what my father was insinuating. "I only come here cuz if I don't *you* gon' blow me up askin' for Ro and Dot," I pointed at my mama as I called her out. "And don't act like you ain't neva pulled up when I ain't come as often as you liked," I continued to remind my mama just how much she loved my company.

"I like being here," Ro tossed out there causing my mama to squeeze him tighter.

"Yeah, cuz you know you ain't gotta clean up shit," I retorted as his he looked up at my mama to back him up. "Nah, don't look at her..." I admonished him as he twisted his lips, knowing not to speak up while I was being serious. "Cuz yo room is exactly how you left it and you gon' clean it up before you touch any food."

"You haven't been doing your chores?" My mama lifted Cairo's chin so they could lock eyes as he dropped his shoulders in silence.

"Nah, he don't—Mani usually do whatchu do and pick up after his ass. You ain't got no maids 'round here, Ro!" I spoke up for Ro.

"Roro, Meemaw and Pawpaw won't get you that new game

if you don't pick up after yourself," she told him sternly as I rolled my eyes to the side, only to see Dot watching me.

Blowing air in her face, she gasped from the shock then smiled. Doing it again, she giggled before burying her face into my shoulder.

"I'll see you tomorrow—"

"Not if he don't clean up," I quickly burst my mama and Ro's bubble as they looked up at me frowning.

"You better take it easy on my baby," she warned as I shook my head.

"Dats da problem now... Everybody givin' him a pass to do what he wanna do," I told her as my mama nodded then shrugged.

"I thought I *did* clean up my room before I left," Cairo told me as my jaw clenched and my eyes cinched. "I'll do it soon as we get home."

His ass know damn well he ain't thought that. Nodding, I didn't want to be a dead horse, plus I wanted to get home before Amani passed out from cramming.

"Okay, baby—I'll make my french toast tomorrow morning, so don't forget to clean up and go to bed on time," my mama told him, only reminding me of how late he stayed up to play that damn game.

In a minute, I'm gone take that shit and hide it. Bring Ro ass back to my generation. When we only had the Sega or the Nintendo and playing outside for most of our childhood.

"And I want home fries too," Cairo requested as my mama nodded her head.

"Ya'll a trip—C'mon, boy," I gripped the back of his head and pulled him towards me as he laughed. "I'll see y'all..."

Ushering Cairo towards the door, I slipped into the kitchen with Dot to get her jello and her car seat. Knowing she was gonna fight tooth and nail not to be placed in it, I had to be swift about it. Plopping a new jello ball into her mouth, it preoccupied her enoguh to strap her in.

"Got da ass," I teased as she whimpered while tugging on the seatbelt straps.

Walking out the kitchen to the front door, I let us out my parents house. By this time Dot was throwing a fit. Baby girl already know she was doing the most because our house wasn't too far from here. Six minutes, to be exact.

"Chandler, c'mon mama," I pleaded with her while searching the backseat for her pacifier. "She ain't have no bag?" I asked Cairo as he shrugged.

"I'on know–She was here without me," he said as I smacked my lips remembering I'd picked my son up from his mama's house an hour prior to coming here.

"You forgot this." I could hear my mama behind me as I turned to retrieve Dot's diaper bag.

"Thanks mama," I draped my arm around her shoulder then kissed her cheek.

"You be nice to my baby," she told me one last time as I groaned loudly, only to get her to laugh.

It worked.

"*Tsk!* Man, he a be a'ight," I told her, like she didn't already know.

Yeah, I was probably the only person, besides his mama, who got on him. But Ro knew how far we went. His ass didn't even get beat like me and Collin and my cousins, back in the day.

"Okay, love ya, Bubba–And tell Mani, we're long overdue for a girls' spa day."

"Already–Ya'll might get dat day sooner than ya think," I said just as I found Dot's pacifier. "Here," I place it in her mouth to stop her crying.

"All that fussin'–"

"Man," I chuckled and shook my head. "She da real spoiled child—"

"That she is," my mama agreed with me as I closed her door to hug my mama again. "Save me some french toast too," I told her as she giggled and nodded. "Now get in da house, woman."

"I'm going!" My mama called over her shoulder as I waited by my door until she was in the house.

"Let's go!" I clasped my hands together before pulling off.

"What y'all gon' eat?" Cairo asked as I grunted.

"Damn, I forgot about dat," my shoulders dropped as I thought about what Amani would have a taste for.

She usually complained about whatever I brought her because she claimed Chicago had the best food and nothing, seemed to satisfy her, here. I won't deny that Chicago had some good spots, but she was shitting on my city with her claim that everything was subpar.

"You know Mani don't like to eat here," Cairo added to my thoughts as I muffed the side of his head causing him to laugh.

"She gon' eat what I bring her," I told him as I made up in my mind to stop at Chic-Fil-A.

Couldn't go wrong with chicken. And that's pretty much how we bonded in the first place. Chicken, fish, and a fat ass blunt.

"I GOTCHU BABY," I kissed Dot's cheek, smiling as she cooed, gripping my shirt tighter.

Something she always did when I wanted to put her into the highchair. Almost like Dot could sense it. Curling her chunky legs into her chest so I had to tussle and pull her legs out.

"C'mon fat mama—Whatchu doin'?" I tried reasoning with Dot as she fought me on the simplist thing.

"She do dis all da time, daddy!" Cairo chuckled as he came to my side, gently straightening her leg out as I quickly dropped her into the seat.

"*Ooouuu!*" Dot balled up both fist, growling as her face flushed red.

"Gotchu!" I teased and pinched her cheek as she continued to frown up at me. "You cut dat out!" I lightly scolded Dot before turning my back to get her diaper bag.

She had couple jars inside and I knew my baby was hungry. Pulling an unused bottle from the side, I unscrewed the lid and added her milk before shaking it up and giving it to Dot. Happy to accept it, Dot tossed her head back as she stuck the bottle into her mouth. Grabbing a handful of her curls with her free-hand, she hummed and drank, in content.

"Eh, eat yo food first and go clean yo room—And watch yo sistah, I'll be right back," I instructed as Cairo nodded his head, already getting his nuggets and sauce from the bag.

Skipping up the stairs, I wanted to pop in on Amani to see how she was doing and tell her I got dinner. As I neared our bedroom, I could hear her frantically speaking and knew she was on the phone. Slowing my pace, I crept to the doorway and hid beside it so I could eavesdrop.

"No he doesn't!" I could hear her scoffing. "No, I'm just saying... I'm not the only thing on his mind," she sighed as my ears perked up to listen even harder. "Brandon is a narcissistic, gaslighting asshole!" Amani roared before laughing.

Hearing that muhfuckas name had my left eye twitching. It's been a year and some months and I thought moving away from Chicago would be the last time he was ever brought up... But I was wrong.

"Shut up!" Amani's voice kicked up in my head, as I tuned

back into her phone conversation. “I'm just don't need y'all thinking I have feelings for that nigga.”

Inching one foot forward, I was ready to make my presence known.

“No, I'm cool,” she stopped me, midway.

Waiting a minute, I thought the coast was clear until I heard Amani sniffling. *Fuck is she cryin' for?* I thought as my face curled with confusion.

“You think I should come up for a visit?” she sobbed. “I miss you guys,” her voice cracked as my face softened. “I think I made a mistake,” she said just as I took two more steps towards the doorway. “I'm not supposed to be here—I don't have anybody!”

Fuck dis! I thought, knowing this was my cue to let Amani know I was here. Walking up to the door, I could see Amani covering her eyes with one hand as she held her phone to her ear with other. Still crying, she usually covered her face, so I knew these were actual tears.

“I was thriving back home—I could've finished school and...” she stopped talking because one of her sisters had interrupted her. “NO!” she blurted out loudly, removing her hand from her eyes. “He went to pick up Ro—With him,” Amani still hadn't noticed me, yet. “You were barely around me!” she was becoming irate and I was close to clearing my throat so she could end the call.

Watching her face go from sad to annoyed as she looked off to the side, our eyes met, and she gasped. Dropping her phone, the color in her face drained.

“Hey, I'm gonna call y'all later!” her voice and attitude did a complete 180 as she nervously ended the call.

Watching her remove her laptop from her lap, she sat her phone on top of it, twisting her lips and staring back at me. She knew I heard their conversation but I could tell by the shiftiness of her eyes she didn't know how much I'd heard. All this time I spent wondering what'd happened between us, was made crystal clear tonight. She no longer wanted to be my wife or stay in Dallas. But Amani had another thing coming if she thought I was about to raise my daughter between state lines... Or let her leave me, this easily.

Going into the bedroom, I waited to see if she'd say something to me... Anything but she didn't. *Figures she wouldn't,* I thought as I kept walking around the corner, into my closet to take my jewelry and shoes off. Giving her some time to get her story straight, mentally, I stood by the closet entry, scrolling through my phone notification. Troy hit me up a few hours ago, and I meant to call him but time got away from me. Texting him back, I stuffed my phone back into my pocket and left my closet to see Amani still in bed, but perched on her knees, waiting for me.

"Hey," she finally spoke to me. "How was she?" She kept talking after I didn't greet her back.

Flexing my jaw, there was one thing I hated more than lying... And that was manipulation. Amani had that shit down bad, if she knew it. And I believe, most of the time, she knew what she was doing. I just loved her, so I let her get away thinking she got over on me... Plus, it was petty shit she used it on me for like what movies we'd watch together or where we'd go to eat. Most of the time, I couldn't decide so I'd let her take charge... But when it came to real shit, like this, I hated it.

"Can you *like* talk to me?" she tried coyly asking and batting her eyes as I glared over at her.

"Are you gon' *like* tell da truth?" The inflection of my voice changed when I copied one of her words as her face curled in confusion. "Then I ain't got shit to say—"

"Carter what—" she grabbed my arm just as I turned to leave. "*Wait*—Why are you acting like this?"

See, what I mean? I hate dat shit!

"Don't do dat shit, Amani," I warned her while snatching my arm from her grip, forcing her to get out of bed to trip after me.

"Do what?" she laughed, and that only pissed me off even more.

Breathing in as I turned to face her, I could feel my body cooking as the heat from my temperament rose. Angrily grabbing her arms, I clenched and shook her a little until I could feel myself calming down. *Don't play with me, Shawty,* my eyes shot daggers into hers as she swallowed slowly. Looking over her beautiful face, I couldn't fathom her not wanting to be here... Shit, not wanting to be with me. I know when we first met, getting married and having a baby was the furthest thing from her radar but I just truly believed she felt what I did. That we'd get through her schooling as a family and she'd be solid—But I was wrong.

Breathing deeply, I released Amani from my grip just as Dot began to cry. *Perfect timing, baby girl,* I thought as I looked away from Amani towards the hallway then back at her.

"We gon' knuckle up, Shawty," I promised her as I flicked her chin, leaving her in our bedroom to think about her next move, wisely.

If she knew better, she'd come to me as my wife and an adult, leaving the games to Cairo and his lil buddies on Fortnite. Shuffling down the steps, I could hear Cairo trying to reason with Dot as she continued to cry.

"Just take yo pacifier, Dot—Daddy finna be down here!"

"I gotchu," I relieved my son of his brotherly duties, pulling the tray from the highchair and placing it on the table. "Go clean yo room."

"I'm already on it!" Cairo shouted from what sounded like the stairs.

"Whatchu lookin' at—Doin' allat cryin' for no reason," I talked to Dot as she watched me before grinning. "Daddy not finna hold you all night," I told her as she blinked and exhaled like she didn't believe the words coming out of my mouth. "You goin' to bed!" I shouted as I spun us around to see Amani coming into the kitchen.

Dropping my smile and my overall mood, I could see her eyes fall after they met the uninviting scowl on my face. Dot could feel the tension too because she started squirming in my arms.

"Okay, Carter, what?" Amani's arms flailed as she made it closer to the island where I was standing.

"Whatchu mean, *what*—I should be askin' yo ass dat shit!"

"So, ask me then!" her tone matched mine and I kinda wished I hadn't taken Dot from her chair, yet.

"C'mon, Shawty—*Say*..." I clenched my jaw as my head shook slowly. "Quit fuckin' playin' wit me."

"How am I playing around? I'm asking you what you're asking me—"

"You doin' dat shit because you already know!" My voice got louder, startling Dot as she flinched a little from the sound of it.

"I already know what, Carter?" Amani was still on games as I swiftly place Dot back into her highchair. "Why are you talking in code?"

Snapping her in, I turned and rushed up to Amani, giving her no space or time to react.

"Was you on da phone when I came in?" I tried to keep my voice low for the kids' sake.

"Yeah with my sisters..." Amani feigned confusion, and I was close to exploding.

"Crying and shit—*Mani*..." I winced, gripping the top of my head because she was driving me up the wall. "Shawty don't—" Pausing just as I caught the look on her face, I knew how to flip this shit on her. "Get da fuck away from me."

Watching her face crack, I knew she didn't expect to hear that. Turning my back to her, I lifted Dot from her highchair and moved towards the hallway.

"Carter what did I say so badly to get you to treat me like this—"

"Mani, you know what I heard and I'm not playin' dis shit witchu—Say how you feel or shut da fuck up—"

"Stop talking to me like that!" She yelled over me just as the tears fell.

Another form of manipulation. I'm all out of tricks and I'm not entertaining this shit. Amani was baiting me so she'd find out just how much I'd heard from her phone conversation. It wasn't even that she did anything wrong but as my wife; I expected her to come to me with any problem. Even if it dealt with her being homesick. She knew I wasn't a monster. I'd make arrangements for her to go see her family and if she wanted to go alone, I'd be cool knowing she was straight with my niggas in Chicago. Torin and Tyrone would make sure their wives' sister stayed safe... So, I knew this shit was deeper than visiting.

Leaving Amani in the kitchen crying, I walked over towards the steps, "Ro, let's go!"

Looking towards the door, I had a pair of Nike slides, I'd have to wear with these socks because the rest of my shoes were upstairs. Slowly making his way to the top of the stairs, I could tell by the look on my son's face that he'd heard everything.

"Let's go—"

"Where we goin'?" he had to asked as my left brow rose, wiping the curious look off his face.

Humping down the stairs, I clutched my pockets until I felt

my keys. Leading the way to the door, I let Cairo step out first then I locked it after I was out the house.

"Shit!" I cursed, after realizing I left Dot's car seat on the countertop. "Don't tell nobody how I'm ridin'," I told Cairo as I got into the driver's seat with Dot still pressed against my chest.

I was only going back to my parent's house anyway, but I'd take it slow... *My kids safety mattered the most.*

CHAPTER THREE

Amani

Staring into the light on my computer screen, I was supposed to be researching abortion for my social issues paper, but I couldn't bring myself to do it. Not for the obvious reasons. *No...* My mind was on Carter and the scene I'd caused last night. Picking a fight just to keep myself from telling him how I was feeling. The childish approach. Which Carter had caught onto and reacted way differently than I'd expected. Leaving me to my drown in my own tears. Taking Cairo and Dot with him, probably to his parents's house or his brother's. Either way, with their tight-knit family... My best bet was to stay in this enormous stucco fortress and wait out my punishment. Because that's what this was. Torture in the worst way.

It's funny though, how quickly my feelings changed. From sulking in nostalgia to hoping Carter would get over this and come home to me. This was utter confusion, and I knew, now, Fatima was right. I didn't need to be in Chicago—I didn't belong. My home was here, but I still needed to get over this hump. Whatever was keeping me in this depressive state of mind.

Bringing my knees up to my chest as I wrapped my arms around them, I exhaled softly. Closing my eyes, I kept my breathing steady so I could clear my thoughts. It was the only thing that seemed to work, lately. Once I felt the calm, I opened my eyes, reaching for my phone to call the only person who listened when I spoke.

"*Heh*—Hello?" Her voice was groggy and I could tell my call woke her.

"Hey, you gotta minute?" I crossed my fingers hoping Torin wasn't at home, yet.

Not that he was as bad as he used to be, towards me, since they got married but he still hated sharing her with us. Especially if he'd been gone all day. He'd annoy her or continue dropping unnecessary comments until Fatima couldn't ignore him and hung up. Childish, yes, but that was Torin Joseph Taylor... *My pettiest brother-in-law.*

"Yeah," Fatima's tone changed as she cleared her throat, probably while sitting up, too. "What's wrong?"

"Everything," I sighed. "But first, I need to apologize," I felt the need to clear the air before I bombarded my sister with my burden.

"Don't even trip," Fatima giggled softly, always so forgiving and lighthearted. "I know you didn't mean to snap at us... Trust me, I do," she yawned. "But how's Dot?"

I wasn't expecting this question so soon after hello but my daughter was the reason I was calling so I had to come out with it. Own my motherless ways and pray Fatima had some gems to toss my way.

"I don't know," my shoulders fell with my eyes as I stared down at the comforter. "She's with Carter—All the time," I braced myself for the admonishing I just knew was coming.

"He takes her so you can focus on school?" She asked me instead.

"Not entirely," I responded truthfully.

"*Mmm,*" she hummed as my brows furrowed.

I didn't know what that was supposed to mean but I was so on the fence about my situation my suspicious made it seem like judgement.

"So, this is deeper than wanting to come back, huh?"

"Yeah," I exhaled deeply, feeling a river of shame wash over me.

"Talk to me then—Tell me how you feel every single day," Fatima suggested causing me to groan. "I mean, you *did* call me to talk, right?" she was playing on my emotions but she was right.

"Yeah, I guess—"

"Okay, so tell me!"

Inhaling, I held my breath as I gathered my thoughts together. There were so many things I kept bottled up and I didn't know which was more depressing.

"I don't feel anything," I blurted out. "Like nothing," my jaw clenched as I waited for my sister to chime in.

When she didn't, I took this as her pulling a Carter, whenever he stayed silent to keep me from going back into my shell. Thus, leaving me no choice but to bare my soul then, and only then, would he give his feedback.

"I know I love Dot but I just can't access those emotions or grasp how I'm supposed to feel when she's with me," my left hand moved as I spoke. "I mean, like, I don't even flinch when she cries and I hate that," I admitted in a huff. "Not that it even matters—"

"Yes, it does!" Fatima cut me off. "Why don't you think it does?" she questioned me.

"Because it's not like I can calm her down when she cries, anyway," I shrugged it off.

"Mani, really?" Fatima's sarcasm was not needed. "It's like that sometimes," she chuckled. "The twins still go through those phases," she told me. "First, they loved me and just didn't want anybody else touching them then *Joseph* became their favorite and now it's like a cross between Nana and Tamika—"

"Torin's mom?" I was shocked to hear this considering how much he loathed her.

And I don't mean like the way he used to despise me and Salimah... No, Torin hated his mother something fierce. You couldn't bring her name up without him cursing you out. That's how bad it was. In fact, the only person who could get him to somewhat respect her or keep a level head whenever she was around was his grandmother.

"Yeah... It's kinda a long story but when Yelly was out here we bonded a lot," Fatima told me as I cringed at the sound of Troy's wife's name.

Not that I hated her or anything but she just had a lot of baggage, when we met and it sort of spilled over into everyone's lives. Including mine. You know when BJ took her in, thus beginning to unraveling of our eleven year friendship. Not to mention when her baby daddy came to Chicago to get her, she turned on my sister and I didn't like that. Fatima may have forgiven her but me and Salimah were still on the fence about Nayelis. And she knew it because there was always this awkward energy between us whenever the Banks family came together for cookouts and holidays. The only reason I remotely tolerated her was for Carter's sake. With him being extremely close to his cousin, Troy, I felt like my small grudge would only cause unnecessary drama between us.

And it's not like she put her hands on Fatima, like she was close to doing with Salimah... She just gave her the cold shoulder and had my baby sister in her feelings, while she was pregnant. It wasn't necessarily her actions but the principal of it all. And her only redeeming factor was the people I loved who loved her or the people close to her. Like Ebony, who was like a sister to me—Well, technically she, considering my marriage to her boyfriend's older brother. Still, Ebony and Yelly were best friends, and I had to play nice for my sister-in-law's sake. But the grudge still stands because nobody messes with my family and gets away with it.

"So, Torin is cool with it?" I had to know.

"Yes and no," Fatima laughed, causing me to crack a smile. "He was furious when I snuck out to have lunch with her and Talib—"

"Why must you always test the waters with him?" I giggled while shaking my head.

"Because, that's the hubby!" I could hear her smiling as she spoke those words.

"You're brave," was all I could say.

"Girl, boo!" Fatima smacked her lips. "One thing I'm not... *Is* scared of that man," she spat confidently. "I'm the only person in this world he'll talk that *fu* shit to then kiss and hug up on in the next breath."

She was right. Torin was a true gemini, crazy and prone to temper tantrums he'd cool down from in an hour or two. Still, he didn't tolerate disrespect from anybody but Fatima. And I wouldn't categorize the little things she did to him as such but I do know, she's the only person who can go toe-to-toe with him and still have him melting like butter in the palm of her hand.

"You forgot about Nana," I tossed in, remembering his favorite person before my sister came into his life.

"Nope, *Joseph* won't even play like that with Nana," she told me. "You know she'll have him bent over her knee," Fatima giggled as I laughed.

"Yeah, she don't play," I smirked remembering the few times I was in her presence with all her grandsons in attendance.

They each held Nana to a higher standard. Something Tamika hadn't achieved with all of her sons, well not back then, at least. With this news of Tamika and my sister getting all chummy together, I didn't know the nature of her relationships with her sons.

"Yeah..." Fatima sighed and just like that the mood shifted.

Back to the negative energy I called her to discuss. Tucking my bottom lip into my mouth, my sister's silence made me nervous. Poking my lip back out, I wanted to bite my fingernails.

Ting. Ting.

Lowering my phone as I tapped the speaker button, I knew this sound. An email, this late screamed spam or worse... A persistent subscription I was going to mark as junk for interrupting my conversation.

"*Hhh!*" I gasped as my eyes ran over the name of the sender.

"What?" Fatima heard me.

Fumbling with my phone, I accidentally ended the call. *Dammit!* Scared to pick it up, my hands started shaking as my mind swirled with ideas of why Brandon would reach out to me via email. I mean, yeah, my phone number had changed and I no longer lived in Chicago... But I thought after the sneaking over to his house and Carter bursting both our bubbles... He'd remain a thing of the past.

"Shit!" I cursed after being frightened from my ringtone. "Hello?"

"Yeah, what happened?"

Of course she'd call back.

"Nothing," I lied for good reason. "I nipped my hangnail in the cover and dropped my phone."

Oh, my God! What is wrong with me? I thought as I shook my head in disappointment.

"*Ugh—Yeah,* I hate when that happens," she bought it. "So, are you still feeling bad or do you need to talk some more?"

My lips fell partially open as Brandon's email hung at the forefront of my thoughts, I no longer cared to get things off my chest. I mean, yes, I wanted to get down to the nitty gritty or whatever was causing this disconnect from my daughter... But that email was more enticing. And I didn't want to do it with Fatima on the phone.

"Don't feel bad—Like it happens," she said when I didn't give her a response.

Dammit!

"I know you probably heard this all before but I promise you..." Fatima paused to put a little emphasis on her words. "*We* all have doubts when we first become mothers—And especially with the way we were brought up... Questioning yourself is a good thing."

What did she just say?

"How is doubting my ability to parent my child a good thing?" I just know I didn't hear her correctly.

"Because, it means you *do* feel and yearn to be greater in Dot's life," she told me as my shoulders dropped and my mouth closed. "Your mind is processing what you lack and you want to do better—*Mani*, I was the same way—Whether or not you believe it... I lived it, too," she told me as my ears perked up. "As crazy as this might sound—I got used to living in my car after that day..." Her words trailed off and I swallowed out of remorse. "You know," she said to remind me of my compliance without brutally berating me. "But when Joseph came along and put me in his penthouse like Rapunzel... I was bored, lonely and missing y'all like crazy," she laughed but I couldn't join her.

The guilt from how I stood idly by while our mother treated her like dirt would haunt me to no end. No matter how well we've managed to come since then... I'd live my entire life feeling like the debt to my baby sister could never be paid—And it wouldn't but I owed her that much.

"It wasn't until we started dating that I stopped thinking about y'all—Then I got pregnant and my hormones went crazy to the point where my doubt of being a better mother than Jewel overshadowed being homesick." Fatima cackled again as my eyes lit up.

There it was! My truth. And Fatima had, in fact, lived it as she said she did. Smirking to myself, I kept my thoughts hidden as my sister continued talking.

"I was freaking out every day—Spazzing out on Torin, feeling like the more I kept my emotions bottled up the further it tore a rift between us and it did but not like how I was thinking."

"What do you mean?" I finally spoke up feeling like her story could very well be mine.

"I mean, yeah, we fought constantly but Torin wasn't gonna let me go—Even if I wanted to get as far away from him as possible and believe me, I tried," she laughed and this time, I did too. "And I did it in the worst way. Meeting up with Retro—"

"From our building?"

"Yeah," she responded quickly. "After I had the twins, I took Mink and—"

"No!" I was in disbelief. "Don't tell me you took him with you to see—"

"Yup, and Torin popped up out of nowhere, scaring the shit outta *us*," Fatima recalled, and suddenly his death made sense to me. "And I'm not gonna lie—I'd started to believe Retro could take me away from everything because I thought the only way to escape my feelings was to run away..." Fatima stopped talking as my thoughts consumed me.

This wasn't some random Chicago shooting. Retro's murder was a message for Fatima and him. *See, this is why I told her Carter was nothing like Torin.* Yes, he changed my number and completely lost his cool, but I wouldn't jump the gun to think he'd kill for me or over me. That's the psychotic gene those Taylors all seem to have. Must've been passed down from their mother. *Oh, Gosh, I hope my sister's kids don't inherit it.*

"Yeah, but I was running from nothing, you know," my sister's voice filled my thoughts as I got out of my head to listen to her. "Torin wasn't the enemy, and I was just scared—"

"Of what?" I could feel my heartbeat racing as I waited for Fatima to respond.

"Losing Tamir and just doubting my ability to raise Mink," she laughed at herself. "I mean, out of the three of us—The mother-daughter relationship never existed," Fatima reminded me as nibbled on my thumb, too guilty to chime in. "She hated me and I've read books on how your mother's rearing unintentionally becomes yours—"

"That's not true!" I blurted out feeling the shame from my own nonexistent bond with my own daughter.

"I know, now... But in the beginning, those thoughts consumed me," Fatima scoffed. "I was a lone wolf, playing house with the kids in tow." She stopped talking briefly then started back up. "With a man whose life could end at any moment—And it almost did!"

"Oh yeah," I added after remembering the car accident and shooting that landed Rico in a wheelchair and Torin in a sling.

"Life's a funny thing though," Fatima giggled.

"How so?" I smiled, wanting to laugh too.

"Because after the shootings—And Torin dragging me out of the restaurant... We fought, and I told him everything," Fatima told me as I mentally took notes. "And I realized I didn't need anybody else to take me away or make me feel whole..." she paused for a moment but I was stuck on that last word. "My kids fulfilled that void and so did Joseph," she boasted and the smile on my face dropped instantly. "My relationship is solid, and I got this mama thing on lock!" Fatima beamed.

"Yeah, you do," I was happy for her, but you couldn't hear it in my voice.

"Is that why you were mad when Salimah asked you about mother's day?" Fatima figured it out.

"Kinda," I sighed with a slight nod of my head. "I don't know what I'm doing—"

"That's normal," she told me what Carter, his mother, and every nurse, who'd come into my room after Dot was born to help me nurse, told me.

"But I don't want it to be," I threw my hand up as I spoke. "I should know, by now, what I'm doing!"

"No, it doesn't work like that—"

"But it should!" I cut her off, grabbing a clump of my hair as I looked up at the ceiling.

I could feel my heart drop to the pit of my stomach as I thought about the times I couldn't calm Dot down or get her to reach for me whenever somebody else was holding her. I even thought about the relationship I had with her brother, Cairo. How easy it was to get him to like me. And part of that liking came from being his father's wife... But Cairo was a cool kid. He didn't ask for much and he always did what I told him to do. *And he was also ten. And I didn't give birth to him nor did I raise him.* The disconnect between me and Chandler could be seen and felt by anybody who'd spent five minutes around us.

"You and Salimah make it look so easy and I feel incompetent compared to—"

"See, that's it right there," Fatima cut in. "You can't compare your life to ours because we're not the same, even though we *are* sisters. Whatever I went through, you didn't and the same for Salimah. No matter what it looks like on the outside there have been moments—I just got through telling you how I used to feel!" Fatima's tone was slightly higher and I could tell she was becoming emotionally overwhelmed. "I may know what I'm doing, now, Mani, but I didn't before—And whose to say I'll always be this confident in my parenting?" Fatima was talking to me like I was her little sister but I didn't mind. "Motherhood is a growing experience, something you'll learn from for the rest of your life—Trust me, I know this firsthand."

The silence that followed was deafening. It forced me to hear every word my sister spoke and apply it to my life. There was no room to ki-ki or switch to another subject—No, I had to face the facts.

"So, when will I start to feel like I'm doing it right?" I spoke up after a few minutes of processing.

"I can't answer that because I'm not you but I do know..." Fatima suddenly stopped talking as I inched up on the bed in anticipation. "*Stop!*" She giggled, and I opened my mouth to speak until I heard lips smacking, more laughter, and whispering. "No—Because I'm talking to my sister!" Fatima's voice rose an octave.

"Man, fuck them," Torin cut her off, in his typical rude fashion.

"It's only Mani on the phone!" Fatima corrected him as I rolled my eyes and scoffed, hoping Fatima had me on speakerphone.

"Fuck her too," he snorted before laughing as Fatima groaned then giggled. "Shit, I'm tryna—"

"You're always *tryna* do it!" Fatima talked over Torin as my face curled in disgust.

I wasn't a prude, but I didn't like hearing about my sisters' sex lives. They were younger than me and I could never picture them in that light. No matter how many kids they had.

Hearing laughter followed by ruffling sounds, I could hear my sister pleading for Torin to stop as she giggled loudly. Kissing sounds and slapping skin, I didn't even want to begin to imagine where could heard too.

"*Eh*, get off da phone," Torin was now louder in my receiver and I knew by the way Fatima cackled that he'd taken the phone from her.

Click.

Dropping my jaw, I should've expected this, but I didn't. Muttering insults underneath my breath, I glanced over to the side and jumped further back onto the bed.

"*Oh, my God—Carter!*"

Slamming my palm to my chest, my eyes scanned his scowling face. *Dang, I really did a number on him,* I thought as my hand fell with my shoulders.

"Where's Dot?" I asked, like any normal mother would.

"Sleep," he responded blankly before turning towards the bathroom.

Getting up, I knew the only way for us to get back to normalcy would be if I apologized. And I dreaded this very thing but I love Carter... And Fatima was right—I couldn't lose him over this. Especially since I was his wife. *No, I'm going to be a big girl and say I'm sorry because we're staying married.*

"Why you followin' me?" Carter called over his shoulder as he flicked on the bathroom lights.

Dropping my eyes in shame, Carter went on like I wasn't even there. Unzipping his pants and pulling himself out for relief. Picking at the skin on my hands as my eyes wandered around the bathroom and Carter, he finished peeing, shaking himself and pulling his pants back up. All without even turning to look at me.

"So, you ain't got shit to say?" He asked as he flushed and slid over to the sink to wash his hands.

Sometimes I hated how vulgar he could be. Everybody in his family, with the exception of his mama and auntie Pamela, cursed like sailors. Collin more than Carter, but excessively nonetheless. And Carter had a vast vocabulary he loved to pair with a *shit, fuck, or ass!*

"Not when you talk to me like that!"

No, Mani, no! That's not how you apologize!

Hearing him breathe deeply, I knew I was messing this apology up. Clasping my mouth shut, I watched Carter dry his hands before cutting the water. Turning around, his eyes were low, which means our argument led to a heavy solo session. Trying not to catch his eyes, I failed. Even in the red, I couldn't resist the green. Same color as our daughter's... I could feel the sadness creeping back up as I thought about how much Dot favored Carter and his granny D. If I loved him so much, why didn't I feel this way towards Chandler?

"Goodnight," he blurted after my continued silence.

Pushing himself off the counter he was leaning up against, my mouth hung in shock. *Is he serious, right now?*

"Carter, really?"

I tried reaching for him as he left the bathroom but missed him by an inch. Stalking through the open space that separated our bedroom from the adjacent walk-in closets and bathroom, I was right on his heels.

"Yeah, Mani, cuz I'm not finna play these games witchu, Shawty—"

"What games?" I cried out as he stopped to turn around.

"Dis shit!" He sliced the air in frustration as he yelled back at me. "You can run ya mouth to yo sisters about any and everything and all dat shit involves me," his palm slammed against his chest. "What is it—You think we made a fuckin' mistake? *Huh*?" He was repeating what I'd said, but he was also jumping to conclusions. "You wanna take yo ass back to Chicago?"

"No!" I quickly shouted out, knowing that's exactly what I wanted to do... Initially.

Then Fatima got me thinking, instead of reacting emotionally. And I wanted to be here. With my husband. I wanted us, the way we used to be... Well, not entirely because Dot was here, now, too—*Oh, my God... I don't even know.*

"*See, man*—Say, Shawty, you do whatchu want," he suddenly lost interest and turned himself back around.

"Carter, no—Okay..." sighed, relieved that he'd stopped walking to hear me out.

God, how do I tell him what I told Fatima? Woud he still love me—Oh my God, of course not! He loves Dot.

"I do miss home..." I started speaking as my brain worked

out the rest of my wording. "I mean... It's a lot," I said for lack of better words. "I'm still processing—"

"And you couldn't come to me with dat?" he asked as I shook my head. "When dat start?"

His second questioned confused me.

"What do you mean?"

"You used to talk to me about everything—School shit, family shit—Anything on yo mind... You called me or waited for me to come home," he reminded me of the days before Dot got here and I could feel a wave of sadness washing over me. "I'm just tryna figure out when you stopped feelin' like you could come to me..."

"I..."

Didn't have an answer for him and he knew it. I mean, I guess I wanted him to be happy without the burden of me pressuring him to go back home. And Carter was overjoyed when I agreed to move in with him... How could I mess this up? We're married now and we have a child together. Moving back to Chicago, let alone visiting, would become a who ordeal. I'd have to pack for me and Dot, figure out if Cairo was coming—Which he probably wouldn't considering the fact that me and his mother didn't speak. We'd have a nice place to stay, up there, but... it wouldn't be the same.

"I'm sorry, baby..." Was all I could say.

"Shit, ain't nothin' to be sorry for—I'm da one who should be sorry," Carter callously turned away from me, heading further into the bedroom as I ran up on him.

"What does that even mean—"

"Don't worry about it," he cut me off while pulling the pillows from the bed and tossing them to the floor.

"Don't worry about it? *Really*, Carter?" I asked as he ignored me, now removing his shirt and pants as I crossed my arms over my chest.

Pushing my laptop towards my side of the bed, along with my phone, Carter was climbing into bed when I childishly pushed him. Fumbling onto the bed, he got up quicker than I'd expected, snatching me up in just as quickly.

"See, why you wanna do dis shit?" Carter huffed into my face, still clutching the front of my shirt to keep me near him. "You just apologized for what?"

"Because I meant it—"

"You ain't mean shit by puttin' yo fuckin' hands on me!" he talked over me as I rolled my eyes to the side. "I'on care bout yo funky ass attitude—"

"Good, I don't care that you don't!" I matched his tone as the grip on my shirt grew tighter.

Yanking me forward, Carter made space for me to fall on the bed as he got up and between my legs. As mad as I was with him, I couldn't deny how much hornier I was, at this very moment. Leaning into me, Carter's lips met mine and instead of pecking he bit them. Something I didn't expect but welcomed by moaning in ecstasy. That did more to me down there than a kiss from him ever did. Wetter and waiting, Carter pulled back to yank my sweats from my body. Wanting to give him a helping hand, I propped myself up to get my shirt off, only for Carter to swat my hands away, so he could do it himself. Pushing me down, he aggressively pulled my legs apart and assumed his position back between them. Pulling my panties to the side, I finally understood that this moment wasn't meant for both of our satisfaction. Yes, I'd get off, but he was doing this to relieve his aggression. *I should've just told him the truth...*

"Wait, wait—Hold up," I pressed my palms to his chest, knowing he'd overpower me. "Carter—"

"*Shit*—Move yo hand," he demanded, pushing his body down on me.

Gazing up into his eyes, he rolled them to the side to keep from looking back at me. That hurt a little because now, I felt like sex was just his way of ending a conversation he didn't want to have. The last thing I wanted was for Carter to develop a habit of doing this to me because ultimately... He'd grow to resent me or worse—We both end up hating each other.

"Get up—Get off me, now!" I slapped his chest harder, hearing him groaning as he moved around then lifted off me.

"*Tsk!* I shoulda neva came back—"

"No, yes you should've!" I cut him off, knowing if we didn't say what was bothering us, there would be no true resolve. "What's really going on—"

"You're one to ask," he scoffed before shaking his head. "I've been askin' you two days, now, Shawty but you stay feedin' me da bare minimum... I can't keep dis shit up," he told me as his shoulders flicked in agitation. "I'm yo husband but I don't know for how long—"

"*What*?" I sat up feeling like I hadn't heard him correctly. "What did you just say to me?"

Scratching the side of his face as he remained silent, I could feel a lump forming in the back of my throat but I couldn't cry. I did enough of that yesterday and most of today... Plus; I didn't want Carter to think I was doing it to make him feel bad about what he'd just said. Even if it was inconsiderately heartbreaking.

"You want a divorce?"

"Don't you?" He assumed his former tone from the bathroom as I shook my head. "Man, quit playin', Mani—"

"I don't want a divorce!" I screamed as my fingernails ate into my palms out of frustration. "I love you—"

"Nah—"

"Yes, Carter, I do!" I kept cutting him off because I could

see he didn't believe me. "I wanted to go back home, but I didn't want to leave you!"

"How much sense does dat fuckin' make, Mani?" he asked me as I shrugged. "Nah, for real... I'm here, fully established with you and our kids—Going back to Chicago, to your old studio is gonna be beneficial for who?" His question was clicking, but I hated the way he said it to me. "You wanna visit? You shoulda said dat shit—I ain't even gotta go, and you knew dat."

"No, I didn't!" I was being truthful with him now. "I thought me wanting to go home, for a while would mess things up—"

"How?"

"Because you're happy with us here."

"What da fuck does me being—*Tsk!* Mani," Carter quickly switched gears. "I'd never keep you here if you ain't wanna stay and you know dat," he stopped talking.

"That's not what I mean—"

"Dats what I got—"

"Carter, I'm really trying to have a serious conversation with you," I whined, hating that he was being so headstrong.

"*Oh, now*, you wanna be serious, Mani?" Carter scoffed condescendingly before shaking his head. "After playin' games last night and tryna carry dat same shit into tonight—"

"I wasn't doing that tonight—"

"So you admit you was on bullshit yesterday?"

Crap, he got me!

"Okay, yeah..." My shoulders felt weighted down by guilt so they fell. "I was and I'm sorry, Carter—"

"I'm not tryna hear dat shit," he waved me off while climbing back into bed.

Still on my knees, I watched him fluff his pillow and lie down like I wasn't hovering over him. Crossing my arms over my bare chest, Carter looked over at me and shrugged.

"You sleep ova there—"

"Carter!" I flapped my hands down, annoyed by the way he was behaving.

Blankly staring over at me, I knew the only way to get him to listen to me was to force him. Climbing into his lap, I slapped his hands away from my body when he tried gripping my waist to move me.

"Stop and listen to me—Carter!"

Now I was grabbing his chin and turning his face, like he'd always do when I refused to look at him. Locking eyes, I saw the sadness he was shielding with anger and I wanted to kick myself. It was never my goal to hurt him and that's what I get for playing stupid games. He was right... As an adult and his wife, I should've just conveyed my feelings and we could've avoided all of this.

But what about the way I feel about Dot? Swirled through my head as I lowered my eyes in shame. This fight about going back to Chicago was like spraying air freshener over funk. And I would have to tell him the whole truth because I didn't want to lose him. *Just not tonight.*

Feeling Carter's finger lift my chin up, I released him, giving a weak smile to keep myself from crying. All I could see was the man I first fell in love with and it broke my heart that he felt like I'd up and leave him.

"I'm sorry... I really am," I apologized again as Carter cupped both my cheeks, swiping the tears from underneath my eyes before pulling my face into his.

"I know you are..." he kissed me and I melted into him. "And I also know you're not tellin' me something," his last words made me tense up, as Carter broke our embrace.

Staring into my eyes, he didn't need me to say anything to confirm his suspicions. My reaction was all the confirmation he needed. Knowing if I played it off, we'd be back to where we started, I kept my eyes on his even though I badly wanted to look away. Breathing heavily, Carter went back to kissing me as he maneuvered with his sweatpants underneath me. Lifting my body up slowly, he tried inserting himself in, only to be blocked by my panties.

Instead of asking me for help, Carter pushed me to my back, snatched my panties off and tossed them. Ignoring my gaze, he lifted my left leg in the air and thrusted inside of me. Gasping from the force and pressure, my eyes closed as he pounded his frustrations away. The tension that once consumed us transferred into kinetic energy Carter, then turned into friction. *I guess we'll work the rest of this stuff out in the morning...*

CHAPTER FOUR

Carter

Jolting myself awake, Dot's wailing sounded like an alarm. Loud and unpleasant. Groaning as I rubbed my eyes, I paused for two seconds to make sure I was fully awake. After the work I put in on Mani last night, my legs needed a minute to wake up. Yawning as my palm slid across the sheets, my neck snapped back and I immediately jumped out of bed. Almost tripping over my jeans as I ran out the room, I looked in on Cairo, forgetting he'd decided to stay with my parents yesterday.

"*FUCK!*" I cursed as I closed his door, running towards the nursery.

The light was on, so I knew Amani was in there with her. Slowing myself down just as I got to the door, I took in a breath then walked through it. Eyes widening as I openly stared at Amani, she was rocking back and forth in the chair, crying as she held Dot in her arms. Dazed and confused, I could see it clearly now. Our marriage was never the issue... Dot was. *Fuck, man!*

Springing into action, I've heard of postpartum depression but seeing it firsthand really fucked me up. I knew I should've listened to my intuition and fought Mani on going back to school so soon after graduating. Dot was barely out of her womb and she wanted to pick another book up. Don't get me wrong, I'm all for her furthering her education and accomplishing all her dreams and goals... But not before her health and family.

"Gimme da baby, Shawty," I calmly stepped up to Amani as she snapped out of her fog, shaking Dot in the process.

Something about hearing my baby girl squeal had me snatching Dot from her mother's arms. Bringing her wet face to my chest, I bounced her gently while kissing the top of her head. It's like a switch flipped and Amani's face contorted until she was scowling up at me.

"Why did you do that?"

"Do what—"

"You're always so quick to take her from me like I'm not her mother!" she yelled as she got out of the rocking chair.

"I never said you wasn't—"

"You don't have to!" She scoffed as she got closer.

Instinctively clutching my daughter, I knew my wife wasn't in her right mind and I would hate to have to hurt her for doing something to Dot. Stepping back, Amani matched every step I took.

"You think I'm Dede, don't you?" I watched her eyes take

on a new shape as they narrowed in my direction. "But it won't be easy for you to take my child from me!" Her words caught me off guard and now I was frowning too. "That's what your family does..." she laughed hysterically. "Have babies and try to control the women you're with and when you can't you take the kids as punishment—"

"Mani, shut da fuck up!" I could feel my neck throbbing as she continued to let this dumb ass shit fly from her mouth.

"No, you shut *the fuck up,* Carter!" She spat back at me. "Your cousin did it to *Yelly*, and you went right along and did it to Dede and if you think you're gonna take Dot from me—I'll kill you!"

Now, I ain't never feared anything or anybody but the way Shawty was staring at me... Eyes all glossy with a speckle of spit hanging out the corner of her mouth—I believed every word she spoke.

"Mani, I swear—"

"I'm trying, Carter!" she burst into tears just as her voice changed. "I am..." she continued to sob as I looked from her then Dot, who'd stopped crying altogether.

I guess baby girl could feel what I felt. Swallowing, I didn't know what else to do in this moment, but I needed to get Amani out of the nursery so I could safely put Dot back into her bed.

"I know, Shawty—"

"You don't!" Amani cut me off as she started backing away from me while shaking her head. "I cry every day—*Every... day,*" her voice strained as tears ran down her face. "When you leave me here and take the kids... You don't know what I'm doing, Carter! You're not here!"

She was right. I didn't know shit. Shawty very well could've been harming herself and I'd be none-the-wiser. Just coming back home, smiling in her face like shit was peaches and cream.

"You're the only person she wants," Amani's gaze shifted from me to Dot. "I can't make her stop crying. I can't change her without making her cry. I can't think about her without wanting to cry, Carter—I hate myself because I don't know why I don't love *her*," her eyes pleaded with me to understand and I wanted to. "My sisters keep telling me the same stupid ass shit —*It gets better*," she moved her head to the side as she mimicked one of her little sisters. "*Oh, Mani, we all went through this—It'll pass*," she groaned loudly as her fists balled up. "I shouldn't feel like this!" she roared. "I know what it's like to have a bad mother and I don't want that for her!" she cried as I took a step towards her, causing Amani to flinch, cutting my next move short. "Don't—"

"Okay," I held up my free hand to assure her I wouldn't come any closer.

"But I don't think I can stop it, Carter and I love you so much—You're gonna leave me and take Dot and everybody's gonna know..." Amani's tears were pouring profusely, and I wanted to console her.

Despite what she thought and felt, I'd never leave her. Especially not during this crucial time in her life. *This was mainly my fault, too.* Because Amani didn't want this, I did, but she accepted it because she loved me. And I'd make it my duty to get her back to herself before we moved on with our lives.

"I'm sorry, Carter," Amani turned towards the door. "I think I do have to go."

Running out the nursery, I started to chase her when I realized I had Dot, wide awake, in my arms. Kissing the top of head, the only thing I was grateful for, in this moment, was how young Dot was so she'd never remember this. And how Cairo chose to stay with my parents, so he'd never get to see this.

"Hey, daddy gotta talk to mommy... I wantchu to stay here and chill," I told Dot as I lowered her into her crib.

Thinking she would have a fit, when she didn't, I couldn't stop the smile from spreading across my face. Sticking her pacifier in her mouth, Dot continued to watch me as I turned her TV on. *A little Disney Plus should do the trick,* I thought as I tapped the app and went straight to Muppet Babies. Slipping the remote into the wall pouch, I turned towards the crib to see Dot's attention on the screen.

"I'll be back," I promised, knowing she didn't care now that her favorite show was on.

Leaving the nursery, I closed and locked the door for her safety. The spare key was in my closet, so I'd be the only person accessible to my daughter, tonight. Looking over the banister, the lights were still off downstairs, which was a relief because it meant Amani hadn't done anything drastic. Heading back to our bedroom, I could see the light from her closet and went that way.

Spoke too soon, I thought as I watched Amani pull clothes from the hangers and stuff them in her bag. She was still crying and talking to herself, which put me at a bit of a standstill. I could come at her from behind and force her to stop, but she wasn't in her right frame of mind. That would only startle her and trigger a greater reaction, probably more horrifying than what I was seeing now.

"Mani, can you talk to me," I made my presence known to her as she flinched then turned to look at me. "*Huh*?" I asked again as she shook her head. "Why not?"

Lifting her shoulders, Amani went back to stuffing her overnight bag. Inhaling deeply, I didn't know if I could get through to her. This wasn't my Amani.

"Baby, c'mon," I'd had enough of handling her with kid gloves.

Stalking over to her, Amani thought she was two steps ahead of me, trying to skip away but I caught her. Holding her in my arms as she squirmed, tirelessly, I could feel myself breaking, as I shook my emotions off.

"Mani—"

"LET ME GO!"

"Stop!" I didn't want to shake her, but it happened as a reaction to her pulling away from me.

Yanking herself back, I tried tugging and fumbled, taking one step and tripping, sending us crashing to floor. Acting fast, I flipped on my back so Amani was still locked into my arms but she didn't hit the ground... I did. The pressure was on me.

"I can't do it, Carter," Amani sobbed on top of me while looking into me eyes.

Sitting us up, I allowed Amani some space to readjust herself in my lap. Still crying, she hugged my neck and carried on as I sat quietly trying to fight off the feeling I'd felt during her explosive episode in the nursery. Clenching my jaw, I could feel it pulsing as my eyes welled up. Hugging Amani tighter just as a tear slid down my cheek, I buried my face into her neck and held her close to me.

This wasn't the picture of happiness and love I had in mind when I first laid eyes on her... But I meant what I told her many times before. She was the only one for me, and that's why she got the ring. And through sickness and health, for better or worse, richer or poorer—I wasn't going anywhere. Every problem she had, I'd work tirelessly to solve it and I think I knew how to fix this one.

"C'mere, get up," I tore my face from her neck, tapping Amani on the shoulder to get her to pull back too. "Stand up, Shawty."

"*What*—Why?"

"We finna go lay down," I told her as I lifted us both up.

Carrying Amani out of the closet, I lied her on my side of the bed and tucked her in. Kissing the top of her head, I turned the TV on and stepped back. Grabbing my arm, Amani looked petrified.

"Where are you going?"

"Lemme go check on Dot and I'll be right back," I told her as I watched her eyes drop to her hands in shame. "Hey, we gon' get through this, together," I lifted her chin with my finger. "You hear me?"

Nodding her head, I leaned in for another kiss, then turned and walked away. Stopping at Cairo's door, I remembered he wasn't in there and kept it moving to the nursery. Touch the knob and twisting it, I'd forgot it was locked.

"Shit!" I cursed realizing I had to walk back into the bedroom to retrieve the key.

Amani was still lying where I left her but she also had the remote in her hand. When she saw me come in, she smiled and I returned the gesture.

"I gotta get somethin'," I told her as she watched me slip around the corner into my closet.

Looking over my shoulder, first, I wanted to make sure Amani didn't follow me. Once I was sure she wouldn't get up, I went into my secret spot and got the key.

"I'll be back," I told her, this time chuckling to myself.

Rushing to the nursery, I unlocked and opened the door to find Dot fast asleep. Should've expected that, considering how early it was. Kissing the top of her head, I checked her diaper and ended up changing her diaper and taking off her sleeper before I left. Dot was a hot sleeper like Cairo had been as a baby. Adjusting the volume on her TV so I could hear her crying on the monitor, I kissed my baby again then left out her room. Closing the door and locking it again, I didn't want to take any chances of me knocking out cold and Amani getting up before me.

Slipping back into our bedroom, I kept the nursery key in my pocket and climbed into bed beside my wife. She was still sad but I could tell she was trying to hide it from me. Pulling her into my arms, I kissed the side of her face, brushing her hair from her eyes so she could see mine.

"Do you think I'm crazy?" She asked me as my eyes widened, causing her to snicker. "No, seriously—"

"No," I cut her off to prevent her mind from wandering off into another dimension of *Am I's?* "You had me a little worried in there when you said you was gon' kill me—"

"I didn't say that, did I?" Amani gasped as I nodded my head up and down, causing her to cover her face as she laughed.

"*Ohhh,* butcha did."

"Stop it," she giggled with me. "I'm really sorry, I didn't tell you sooner, Carter... I just didn't know—"

"How to come to me about this—I get it," I told her as she twisted her lips with uncertainty. "I do," I tried convincing Amani that I understood but she wasn't buying it.

"Do you really?"

"Yeah—"

"So, now you understand why I was calling my sisters and confiding in them and not you?" She asked me as I inhaled slowly, causing her to laugh.

"*Yesh.*" Was my tight-lipped response as Amani giggled.

"*Yesh?*" She repeated as I nodded.

"And I was wrong to be mad at you," I told her, seriously as she nodded her head. "*Howww-everrr,*" I extended this word keeping Amani laughing. "You were wrong, too."

"For not telling you—"

"*Ding, ding, ding!*"

"I know and I'll try not to let my thoughts get the best of me," Amani promised me but I knew she was just talking.

It was in her nature to worry and overthinking things. That's just the kind of woman I married. But it was my job to pull her from her thoughts, so we can work through whatever trouble came our way.

"I love you," I kissed the side of her face as she smiled.

"You always beat me to it," she giggled. "But I love you, too and thank you for being so understanding—"

"Oh, but don't thank me too quickly," I cut her off, smirking.

"Why is that?"

"You'll see, come Monday."

"What's Monday?"

"Don't worry bout it—Matter fact, I gotta make a call... I'll be right back," I told Amani as I released her from my arms to get out of bed.

"Where are you going—"

"Don't worry bout it," I repeated as Amani sat up. "Lay back down—"

"Carter!" She snickered, trying to swing her leg off the bed, only to be stopped by me.

"Lay yo ass down—Lemme make dis call," I told her as she frowned up at me. "Hey," I pointed in her face as the side of her mouth quivered. "You already skatin' on thin ice for makin' threats—I'on just let a muhfucka tell me they finna kill me and shit just be breezy."

"Is that a threat?" Amani challenged me.

"Take it how you want it," I countered as she finally broke and smiled, lying back down. "Yeah, dats what I thought."

"You better hurry up!"

"Don't rush me, woman!" I called over my shoulder as I got out the bedroom.

Going to Cairo's room, it was close enough to the nursery and far from my room to do what I needed to do. Plus, if Amani came looking for me, I'd hear her.

"*Hello?*"

"*Eh,* nigga, you sleep?" I held in my laughter, already knowing the answer to my question.

"*Tsk! Man,* whathcu think?"

Doubling over, I could hear Troy groaning as I calmed down to get serious.

"I need that number to ole girl's office."

"The shrink?"

"Yeah—"

"You coulda asked me dis shit later!" He complained.

"Yeah but I need it now."

"Why?"

"Don't worry about it," I puffed my chest out then exhaled, laughing. "Nah, I'll tell you later, nigga—You can go back to sleep."

"Yo ass play too much," Troy grumbled before ending the call.

Not too soon after the call ended, Troy texted me the info I asked him for. Saving the number, I set a reminder to call when I woke back up. *Hopefully, Dot slept a little longer, so I could get some rest.*

CHAPTER FIVE

Amani

STARING AT THE TWO PIECES OF UNBUTTERED TOAST flaking on my plate, I didn't have the desire to touch them. Food was the last thing on my mind, despite the continuous growling of my stomach. I skipped dinner last night too because I couldn't stop obsessing over Carter's surprise. He told me it'd be in our best interest to see it through, and it hasn't sat right with me since.

If that wasn't suspicious enough, Carter had been waking up early, every day this week to take the kids to his parents. Leaving me to my schooling and this empty house. Well, not entirely empty because he'd come right back and bug me then go downstairs, in the front room, to watch TV. Then we'd have lunch, and he'd try to get me to open up about my emotions and what not... To which I'd keep the conversation lite, focusing solely on the semester ending and possibly taking a break. I did, however, throw him a bone, saying I didn't plan on signing up for next semester. Instead, I suggested we take a family vacation or have that honeymoon we neglected because of Chandler being a newborn and me having to graduate.

He liked the idea, but kept waving his surprise in my face without hinting to what it was. Claiming, after, and only after I knew about it would I be ready to take a family trip. *Whatever that means—*

Beep. Beep.

The alarm system chirped, alerting me that the front door had been opened and closed. Perking up on the stool I was seated in, along the island, I didn't want to seem too gloomy. Even if that's how I felt.

"*Mani*? Where you at mama?"

I could hear his clunky shoes scuffing the marble as he slid his feet while walking. Something I always reminded him not to do. *Pick up your feet when you walk!* I shouted internally as his footsteps grew louder.

"Shawty—*Tsk!* Why you not dressed?" He came into the kitchen setting a deli bag on the island.

"*Becauseee...*" I dragged the word a little as I turned to the side. "I was thinking, maybe we could—"

"Nope," Carter shook his head quickly. "Get up," he grabbed ahold of my arm, lifting me from the stool.

"But what if I don't like the surprise?" I groaned as he led us out of the kitchen.

Stopping just before we got to the steps to clutch his chest with his free hand, my toe tapped out of frustration. Smirking because he was being silly, I had to follow up with a roll of my eyes to let Carter know I wasn't in a laughing mood.

"*Ouch!*" he feigned hurt, and I almost laughed but I caught myself.

"I'm being serious, Carter!" My voice was whiny as Carter lowered his hand from his heart to raise his shoulders, like he didn't understand where my reaction was coming from.

"I am too—How you gon' say some shit like dat?" he criticized as I shrugged, wishing he'd just tell me whatever this surprise was so I wouldn't say anything bad about it.

"No, you're not—See, that's why you're smiling!" I pointed up at his face as he doubled over laughing. "Carter, I really wanna take it easy today—"

"*Tsk!* Relax, shawty," Carter quickly cut my attempt to get out of leaving the house short. "We ain't finna be outchea doin' nothin' crazy—"

"So, why can't you tell me so I can mentally prepare myself—"

"Nah," he chuckled as my lips pursed together. "Don't do dat shit."

Trying to cross my arms over my chest, Carter still had my right arm in his grasp and he playfully yoked it to prevent me from physically closing myself off to this conversation.

"C'mon, so you can get dressed—"

"I am dressed!" I protested as he ignored me all the way up the stairs and into our bedroom.

Going into my closet, Carter ushered me through first, releasing my arm from his grip. Looking back at him, he nodded for me to get moving and that's what I did. I mean, what choice did I have? Rifling through my clothes, there was too much to choose from but I knew what I felt like wearing. Sweatpants and a hoodie. Not my signature but since I couldn't lounge around at home, I'd express it through today's outfit.

"No," Carter shook his head as I lifted the clothes I wanted.

"*What*—How can you say no?"

"Cuz you not wearin' dat—Pick somethin' else!"

"Like what?" I matched his tone, catching a serious glare from him.

"Somethin' bright and happy," he suggested as I frowned then rolled my eyes. "Somethin' dats gon' keep me from knockin' you out—"

"I wish you would!"

"Don't tempt me, Shawty... You already threatened to kill me—"

"How many times are you gonna bring that up?" I sighed heavily as my arms flailed in agitation.

"As many times as I see fit," he retorted as I fought the urge to smile.

Turning back to my clothes, "Don't make me take you up on it," I mumbled lowly.

"Dats two—"

"*What*—"

"*Three*!"

"Carter!"

"*Four*—You tryna go for five?" He held his palm towards me as I giggled and shook my head. "Then turn yo ass around and pick somethin' nice—I'ma be out here. You got ten minutes—"

"That's not enough time—"

"*Ten...* Minutes!" He repeated, shouting over me as I groaned loudly.

Ignoring my pouting, Carter walked out of my closet,

leaving me to decided what was bright and happy enough for his liking. *I'll give you bright and happy, alright—*

"*FIVE!*"

"I didn't say anything!" I yelled back at him.

"Yeah, butchu was thinkin' it!" He shouted as I giggled.

He was right! Taking a deep breath, I kind of understood why he wanted me to dress happy. It'd change my mood. *Alright, Carter, you get your wish... again.* I thought as I pulled a frilly, neon pink sundress. The happiest of all my clothing and probably the brightest. Holding it up a small smile spread across my face.

Tossing my shorts and tank off, it took me no time to get dressed. Finding a nice pair of sandals, I wrapped my hair into a bun and gave my makeup a try, today. Mascara and a little lip stain made my gloss pop. Making sure my ring was centered, I added earrings and a few gold necklaces to this ensemble before twirling at my reflecting in the mirror. *Okay, I did look good.*

"Bright and happy—Look atchu!" Carter startled me as he came back into my closet smiling. "Beautiful, now let's go!"

"Can you tell me on the way there?" I poked as Carter shook his head.

"Hold up," he stopped me as we got to the front door. "I gotta get dat food—"

"I'm not hungry," I interrupted just as my stomach growled.

"Somebody else begs to differ," Carter poked my stomach as I giggled like the Pillsbury Dough Boy.

Impatiently waiting, it didn't take Carter long to appear back in the hall, this time holding the deli bag he came home with. I'll admit, he knew me well when it came to eating... And I was curious to see what he picked up.

"You can eat in the car," he told me as if he could read my thoughts.

Opening the door, Carter grabbed my hand and led us through. Being the gentleman he always was, Carter didn't get in the truck before me. Making sure he held my door and handed me my seatbelt. He was the same with the kids. A true protector... I had taken that quality about him for granted, but never again.

"Already!" Carter announced as he got in, clasping his hands together. "Let's roll!"

Grabbing the deli bag, I pulled the cartons from inside, hoping wherever we were going wasn't something I'd hate. Especially with the way I'd been feeling. The last thing I needed was a concert or a group of people parading in my peril.

Reading the sign near the entryway, I turned towards Carter scowling. *A shrink?* He had to be kidding. I didn't need to see a therapist. I wasn't crazy.

"Why are we here?"

"To get help—"

"I don't need help!" I was on the fence already.

Inhaling, Carter didn't dignify my words with a proper response but I would not let up. I mean, I'd asked him if he thought I was crazy and he told me no. Now, I can see he was lying to butter me up to this... This *bullshit!*

"Mani, we need a medium, somebody who won't be bias—"

"So, use your mother or father," I interjected, not wanting to hear his logic on this.

"And hear you complainin' about how my family is all up in our shit, every time you cop an attitude with me—Nah, I like this option better," Carter countered as I rolled my eyes. "Look, it's not as bad as you think—"

"No, but I know somebody who has and these women do great work," he tried convincing me but I couldn't get off the person he knew who'd come here.

"Who do you know whose been here—"

"Troy... And Nayelis," he told me flat out as my eyes widened. "And they helped them like they're going to do with us."

I couldn't stop thinking about Nayelis having postpartum. *She's going through the same thing.*

"Yelly was like me?" I asked as Carter shook his head, quickly cracking my image of what could've been.

"They're therapist, so you can come here for anything—"

"So, that means they don't specialize in what I'm going through," I was back to fighting Carter on this.

"How do you know?"

"Because if people come here for anything, then I'd assume my situation isn't as popular—"

"Only one way to find out," Carter cut me off while doing the same to the engine. "Besides, they're women—Black women, at dat."

"What does that have to do with getting me the proper help, I need?"

"It has everything to do with what you need," Carter told me as he got out.

Watching him walk over to my side to open my door, I undid my seatbelt and took his hand.

"Not only are these women but they're black so they're less incline to take what you say as frivolous emotion. Your lives could very well be parallel just because we're black and that matters in the medical field. Coming from a place of familiarity so you can get a better diagnosis and treatment. And if you need a lil somethin' extra to calm you down... They won't mark you an addict," he told me as we walked, hand-in-hand, towards the entrance.

"I'm not taking any medicine," I told him as he shrugged.

"It's just the principal of it all, Mani... And look," Carter got my attention as he held the door open for us. "You support black businesses in the process," he smiled while holding up his right fist as I giggled. "Now, c'mon, let's do dis shit!"

"You were doing so well," I groaned at the last part.

"Yeah, well, you know I gotta squeeze it in somewhere," he pointed out his ability to curse in any circumstance.

"Oh, I know," I smirked as we approached the front desk.

"Hello, how are you two beautiful people, this mornin'?" The receptionist was off to a good start as my smile brightened before I glanced over at Carter to see him gushing and snickering.

"Stop it!" I shoved him as all three of us laughed.

"Nah, I'm playin'—We gotta appointment with Dr. Clark," he put on his serious face.

"Carter and Amani Banks?"

"*Tis we,*" he nodded as the woman in scrubs giggled.

"Okay, you're early but that's an excellent thing," she twirled in her chair picking up papers and a clipboard. "Just fill these out and Dr. Clark will see you—If you don't get done before I call you, just finish during your session."

"Already," Carter took the clipboard and my hand and led us to the empty seats by the window.

"*Can I get a window seat... Don't want nobody,*" Carter stopped singing to push me away from him as I giggled. "*Next to meeee!*"

"Be serious," I playfully scolded him as he nodded, wiping the smile from his face.

"Alright, so..." Carter cleared his throat as he looked down at the papers we had to fill out. "*Name—*"

"Carter!"

"*A'ight, a'ight, a'ight*—I'ma be serious," was the last thing he said before he got to scribbling on the pages.

Looking over his shoulders, I was shocked to see how much he knew about me. I mean, I know I told him everything but most of the time I thought I was running my mouth and he was barely paying me dust.

"How'd you know—"

"Cuz I listen," Carter talked over me, causing me to laugh. "But I can't say da same for you—"

"*Wuh*—I know a lot of stuff about you," I was not about to sit here and let him do me like that.

"A lot is almost and *almost doesn't count*," Carter held his nose in the air as I continued laughing. "And I know everything —*Well*, I will know everything after you answer dis question, right here," he pointed to the number, on the paper, he wanted me to fill out.

Smiling as I took the pen and clipboard from him, my eyes narrowed in on the question. *Are you pregna*—Smacking my lips as I tossed the board back at him, Carter doubled over laughing as I tried not to join him.

"*Well—*"

"No!"

"A'ight, no need for violence," he playfully scoffed, and I laughed. "*Geeze!*"

Finishing up the rest of the paperwork in silence, I had a moment to my thoughts. And they weren't positive. I mean, yes, Carter raised some great points but I was still on the fence about therapeutic help. I mean, it just wasn't something I believed I needed... Not to mention, I doubt it'd work for me.

Plus, I felt better after Carter and I talked the night I exploded. If that wasn't a breakthrough, I don't know what is.

"Hey," Carter's finger lifted my chin up, pulling me out of my thoughts. "We're doin' dis."

"But I—"

"Mani," his stern tone and gaze let me know there was no room for backpedaling.

"Mr. and Mrs. Banks," the receptionist called to us as we looked her way. "Dr. Clark is ready for you."

"C'mon," Carter helped me from my chair, keeping my hand in his, he led me as he followed behind the receptionist.

"Alright, you two, this is where you get off," she bowed her head towards the door and Carter opened it up for us. "They're all yours, Dr. Clark.

"Hello!" Dr. Clark stood from her chair, extending her hand to shake each of ours. "Thank you, Kimmy!" she dismissed her receptionist while closing the door. "Have a seat —Get comfortable," Dr. Clark directed our attention to the loveseat up against the wall. "Anybody pregnant?"

That question had Carter's eyes on mine as I rolled them.

"No," I answered again, knowing he'd still see this as a sign of some sort and continue questioning me until I peed on a stick in front of him.

"I'm asking because I have french press, if you're interested," she offered as I shook my head, declining. "*Hubby*? You?"

"*Uh*—Nah," Carter rejected her offer as well.

"Okay, then, let's get started..." Dr. Clark went to the other side of the room, grabbing her glasses, a yellow notepad, and a pen.

Looking around the room, Dr. Clark orange painted walls were different. I don't know what mood they intended it to convey, but it confused me. Still keeping my uneasy thoughts about coming here, in the first place, I read some of her achievements and plaques. She was overly qualified but I guess that's a good thing... *Right?*

"*So...*" Dr. Clark cleared her throat to bring me back to earth.

Now sitting and smiling in the chair she was in when Carter opened the door, I didn't return the gesture. As a matter of fact, I frowned, just to show her what I truly thought about her practices.

"You don't like being here, I get it," Doctor Clark giggled as she lowered her frames. "It's normal—"

"*Ugh...*" I loathed hearing that expression come out of her mouth.

I'd heard it so many times before and I didn't need to hear it now. Especially not from a head doctor.

"Okay, we're off to a start—Why the groaning?" She asked as she picked up her pen and notepad, again.

"Because I don't want to be here—"

"*Mani*!"

"*Carter*!" I called out his name since he wanted to act like he was my daddy.

"Alright, let's try a fresh approach..." Dr. Clark could sense where this moment was headed and quickly intervened. "How did you two meet?"

She can't be serious...

"Who wants to start?"

She is!

"I'll start," Carter removed his arm from behind my head as I rolled my eyes over at him for even entertaining this madness. "I saw Shawty ass, across da club while I was blowin' and shit and she wanted a hit—"

"Carter!" I shrieked from his wording more than the truth of how we met.

"Whatchu want me to make some shit up—"

"No, I *prefer* you to not be so crass when you tell it," I scoffed as he smacked his lips.

"Smokin' in da club and fuckin' right after is far from *genteel* but you tell it since you wanna police everything I say," he clasped his hands together as he scooted back leaving me flabbergasted by his words.

"That is not how it all happened!" I stated, hating how he left out the part about me going through my bouts with Brandon and spilling my heart out to him.

Drinking, talking, and smoking while talking some more. Then we had unbridled sex, and he fell madly in love with me. It took me a couple days to come around to those same feelings but yeah, the way he's telling Dr. Clark will definitely have her writing me off as crazy.

"So, why don't you tell me, Amani..." Dr. Clark eagerly held her pen to paper as I looked over my shoulder to see Carter smiling back at me.

Dang it! He got me good!

CHAPTER SIX

Carter

Pulling into my parents's driveway, my phone buzzed just as I parked. It was Amani telling me she cooked. Smirking, I sent a message back to let her know I was on my way. Two sessions in and Amani has shown tremendous improvement. She wasn't as eager to hold Dot, but she lingered around when I fed her and changed her. Laughing at her cooing and babbles whenever Dot held her attention. And that was more than she used to. Really, I was just glad to see her genuinely smiling, like she used to do. Rising early, on most mornings, she took on the day with vigor and I could see she wanted to get better. Not for me but for herself.

Popping my locks, I got out, skipping steps until I was opening my parents' front door. Zipping past me, Cairo and Desmond's youngest Dahir almost crashed into me. Grabbing ahold of my son, he squirmed and wiggled, trying to break loose.

"Lemme go, Daddy!" He shouted just as Dahir tapped his shoulder. "Aww, man!" he smacked his lips, and I released him. "Why'd you do dat?"

"Cuz yo ass know better than to be runnin' in da house—Take dat shit outside!" I scolded both of them as Dahir's big brother Diggy walked up behind them, shaking his head.

"Wussup uncle Carter," Diggy held his palm out to shake up.

Smirking, I slid mine across, locking my index finger to his before releasing it to slide my hand back. Looking and acting just like his daddy, I had flashbacks of the times me and Troy used to tear through our Big Mama's house after Desmond warned us not to. It'd always result in us getting a beat down... And Desmond shaking his head like he wasn't a kid too.

"Whatchu doin' here?" Desmond came out into the hallway, holding Dot and smiling.

"Nigga, I used to live here!" I chuckled as I walked up to meet him.

Soon as Dot was close to me she grabbed ahold of the hand I used to shake up with Desmond. Laughing, I took her into my arms, kissing the side of her face. She couldn't wait to be near me. That's something I'd never get tired of. I'm all baby girl needed.

"She's beautiful, cuz," Desmond complimented my baby Shawty as I nodded my head, beaming. "How's Mani?"

"Good, man—Tryna finish dis semester," I told him without divulging all the other shit we were currently going through.

If I didn't know any better, I'd say my mama had been

talking to him because Desmond rarely asked about my wife. Not that he didn't care, but he was the same with Troy. If there was no problem to fix, Desmond usually minded his business.

"Dats wussup," his entire demeanor changed, going from college prep to south of Kiest boulevard. "Anything y'all need, nigga, I gotchu."

Nodding my head slowly, Desmond shook up with me again then called to his sons and left. *Now I see what Troy was saying,* I chuckled to myself as I walked into the den. Desmond only came back to his true self when he thought it would appeal to one of us. I don't know what the fuck my mama told him or what he thought but me and my wife were good.

"Hey, *Bubba*!" My mama saw me first, alerting my father to my presence.

"Hey son!"

"Don't *hey bubba*, me!" I cut my eyes at my mama as she looked around confused. "C'mere," I sat Dot in my father's lap and she immediately burst into tears. "I'll be back, Shawty—Wussup Daddy," I dapped my father before I walked over to where my mama was sitting to help her move faster.

"Stop—Wait!" she giggled as I pulled her into the hallway. "Why are you acting like—"

"Whatchu been sayin' bout me?" I cut to the chase as my mama's cheeks burned. "Tell me now cuz I'on like—"

"You don't get to question me, Carter!" Megan put on her stern voice as I shifted my eyes to the left. "I was just asking around—"

"For what?"

"Cairo came to me about your big fight with Amani," she stated as I jerked my shoulders indifferently.

"I fight with his mama all da time—"

"And he tells me that too but he also knows you don't love

his mama," she told me as my eyes cinched. "Is there something going on between you two?"

"Nah," I shook my head and watched my mama's head tilt to the side. "I can't argue with my wife or somethin'?" I was trying to understand where she was getting at.

"I didn't say that, but he was scared that you—I don't know maybe it was a bit explosive and you know how children perceive things," she changed her words around but I still wasn't getting it.

"Whatchu tryna say?"

"Maybe he thought y'all were gettin' a divorce—"

"Dat ain't gon' neva happen!" I scoffed with a shake of my head. "Cairo heard one fight, and he came runnin' to you—Nah, whatchu need to do is stop lettin' him run his mouth," I admonished my mother as she rolled her eyes. "Nah, don't do dat... Cuz dis shit gon' always be misconstrued if it's taken out of context."

"I told ya mama!" I heard my daddy yelling as I smirked. "She's too involved in you and ya brother's relationships!"

"Oh, Solomon—"

"Nope... Let them boys handle their own problems—If Eb and Mani come to you, send em back to Bubba and Lin!"

"Straight like dat!" I piggybacked my father's edict as my mama narrowed her eyes at me.

"You hush—"

"Daddy, mama threatenin' me!" I called out as she giggled and raised her hand like she would hit me. "Eh," I caught Cairo trying to ease past me. "You quit comin' to my mama bout me," I eyed him as he nodded his head. "Ya'll spendin' too much time together," I flicked his head as my mama cackled. "I'm finna separate ya'll—"

"You better not!"

"Try me—" This time she did hit me, twice as I laughed

and ran back into the den. "A'ight lil Shawty, let's go home to mommy," I lifted my baby girl from my father's lap as she kicked her legs like it would help her into my arms quicker.

Laughing, she balled my shirt into her first, pulling her face into my chest as I turned to leave. Nodding for Cairo to follow, he hugged my mama and yelled his goodbye to my pops.

"Oh, shit, I almost forgot, mama," I turned around as her eyes lit up. "How you feel about a lil soiree?" I asked, watching a smile spread across her face.

"What type of party are we talking?" She wanted the details.

"Something you been askin' for a while—"

"*Oh,* my goodness—*Yes*!" My mama clapped her hands together. "I know just who to call and where we can have it!"

"Nah, I wanna do it at da crib," I cut into her fantasy, watching her face drop.

"In the backyard?" She didn't like that idea too much, but I already knew what I wanted.

"Yeah—We can host it in tents and shit," I told her as the spark in her eyes flared up.

"Okay—Alright..." she nodded slowly coming around to my idea. "Is it a lite affair?" She asked as I nodded my head.

"I'll be back some time dis week with a list of people," I confirmed as my mama nodded her head.

"I can work with that!" She was excited, and I was too.

"Yeah, give her something constructive to do," my daddy came into the hallway to mess with my mama as I laughed.

"Hey, dats whatchu gotta do to keep her occupied," I pipped in, watching my mama swat at my daddy, next. "I'll catch y'all later," I called out, throwing my arm around Cairo's neck and leading us out the door. "You bet not repeat none of dis shit to Mani," I warned as he nodded his head. "You gotta learn da code, Ro—You a Banks, ain't you?"

"Through and through," he stated while poking out his chest as I smirked.

"Then play yo part," I said as we got to my trunk.

"THAT WAS GOOD, MANI," Cairo belched while rubbing his stomach, causing Amani to giggle.

"Thanks baby—I'm glad you liked it," Amani gushed.

Skipping out the dining room, that boy couldn't wait to get back to his game. Shaking my head as Amani got up from her chair, she began clearing the table. Watching her move around, she didn't notice me looking until she came to Dot's highchair. Clenching my jaw out of habit, Amani grabbed the empty bottle from Dot's mouth, replacing it with her pacifier. And she managed to do this without making her cry.

Turning towards me, her eyes sparkled as her smile widened. That alone had the corners of my mouth curling up. Without saying anything, Amani took the dishes into the kitchen and I could hear them clanking together as she loaded the dishwasher. Taking that as my cue to get up from the table, I came over to Dot's highchair to get her out.

"It's time for bed, Shawty," I kissed her forehead as she whimpered a little. "Nah, nah, nah..." I shook my head, hearing her soft cooing as we walked to the stairs and up them into the nursery.

Sniffing the folds of her neck, she always smelled sweet, but I was still going to put her in the bath. It helped her fall asleep faster and made for a good night's rest.

"Hey," Amani popped into the nursery, drying her hands on her hoodie. "I ran her water."

"You what?" I snapped my neck in her direction as she giggled.

"Stop it," Amani smirked, coming to my side as I finished undressing Dot. "Can I join you?" She asked like Dot wasn't her child, too. "What?" Amani shifted her weight her other foot as she nervously looked around.

"Why you askin'?"

"So, I can't—"

"Mani," I cut whatever thoughts she had brewing in her mind as she nervously snickered. "*Here*," I placed Dot into her arms and motioned for her to lead the way.

Eyes widened with shock and visibly disoriented, chunky Dot hit different in nothing but a diaper. She was softer and slippery and for some reason she squirmed way more without clothes on.

"C'mon," I told Amani as she managed to get a grip on Dot, taking one step then two until we were out the nursery.

Going into our room, around the corner and into the master bath, Amani had the right amount of water in the tub. Nodding my approval, she giggled softly, showcasing a hidden talent as she unhooked Dot's diaper while walking up to the tub.

"*Oh my God!*" Amani shrieked, causing me to run up on them.

"What is it?"

"She peed on me!" Amani's face crunched as she peeled Dot from her side to reveal a puddle on piss.

Laughing, Dot was smiling and cooing with me. *Welcome to da club, Shawty,* I thought as I took baby girl from her hands. Gently placing her into the sudsy bath, Amani got on her knees, grabbing the towel and soap. Allowing her to lead, I crouched down beside her in silence. Overseeing the entire lather up. It was like it used to be when Dot got her first bath and Amani was so eager to clean her up. Dot was uncharacteristically calm, and it made me wonder when it all changed. I'm not questioning her postpartum... I just don't remember the signs. There's supposed to be red flags—*Or maybe I was too blind to see them.*

Then it hit me... Every day was a sign. Amani holding her less or plopping Dot into my arms whenever she cried or couldn't calm her down. Me jumping up at night to get her bottles or change her. I was doing everything, not realizing those moments were a cry for help. I should've shared my parental duties with her. Maybe then, it would've opened her up or allowed me to see she wasn't adjusting to motherhood, like I'd thought.

"Carter," Amani tapped me as I shook myself, falling on my ass in the process.

"Oh, shit."

"You okay?" Amani asked as she helped me up.

"Yeah... My bad," I chuckled before scooting closer to the tub.

Dot was back to herself, splashing water everywhere and laughing. This was the wild child I knew. Splashing her back, Dot's closed her eyes tightly, keeping her mouth open as she squealed laughing.

"She's so silly," Amani cackled as Dot slammed her baby fists into the water, dousing us. "Just like you!"

"She's a Banks," I splashed Amani as she returned the favor. "*Aw*, you wanna play?"

"No!" She fanned her hands in front of her as I got up, squatting down to lift Amani in the air. "PUT ME DOWN!"

"A'ight—"

"CARTER DON'T!" Amani screamed as I hovered her body over the tub.

By this time Dot was all for it. Matching her mama's screams, she splashed more water, giggling as I played like I was going to drop Amani in with her. If Dot was out, then I would. She knew that too. Pulling her back to me, I wrapped Amani's legs around my waist, and kissed her. Slowly letting her down, Amani's eyes never left mine. Those big brown eyes were the first thing you noticed when you saw her. They were huge, slanted, and doll-like eyes. Dot had the same shape, she just had my eye color. Matter fact, all her sisters had the same eyes... It must've been a gem from Jewel.

Paired with her bushy brows, she kept shaped, and her big hair. *How could I not notice her?* And Amani was such a wall-flower, I found myself intrigued the moment she walked in behind Tyrone and his girl. Quietly scanning the surrounding vibes, I knew the crowd threw her off. It took me fifteen minutes to come around and five to get her smiling. But once I did, she was taking my blunt from me, telling me jokes and shit. I thought I was a funny nigga but Amani was definitely the comedienne.

"Stop looking at me like that," Amani blushed as she turned her attention to Dot in the bathtub.

Closing my eyes for a second, it transported me back to Brunner's. Shit was lit as soon as we stepped through the doors. Travis cracking jokes as Torin chuckled, rolling a blunt and shaking his head. Thick as thieves, like me and Troy. Tion cooly seated behind all the action, keeping a watchful eye over his brothers with his right hand, Fredo, smoking beside him, occasionally leaning in to say something that would get Tion's head nodding. Then the back door opened, bringing in the icy chill Chicago was known for during the wintertime. Coming through was the second Taylor brother, Tyrone. Shaking the cold off as a few of the niggas near the door shook up with him.

Watching him look over his shoulder, two ladies filed in not two seconds after him. The first red-haired and clearly agitated. Folding her arms as soon as she stepped inside. And Ty yanking them down just as she crossed them over her chest. *There she was.* The second woman. Dressed in black with hair, the same color, slicked down her back. *Miss Mary Mack.* I had the blunt dangling from my lip as I watched her scoot away from Ty and the redhead. Clasping her hands together and rubbing them for warmth, Shawty coolly slid to the bar, said three words and left with a glass in her hand. Headed my way, my jaw clenched just as the blunt fell to the floor.

"Look at buddy ass fumblin' shit!" Travis couldn't wait to laugh as I grinned, shaking my head.

Too cool for a rebuttal. Amani passed right by us, not turning to speak or even wave. Looking over my shoulder, I watched her slide to the other side of the room until she was seated, alone, nursing the glass in her hand.

"Man, why dis nigga even bring nem?" Torin was the first to state his disdain.

"Who?" I asked, wanting to get Shawty in the back name.

"My baby mama sisters," he huffed while lifting the lighter to the blunt in his mouth.

"Just cuz you like to keep *Fatty Ma* chained up in yo chambers don't mean every nigga gotta move like you," Travis said as he took the blunt from his brother's fingers.

"Man fuck you!" Torin laughed with me and Travis. "I'on keep her locked up—Shorty be gone!"

"Yeah, gone up da street and back—"

Watching the two of them double up, laughing, I stepped away just as Tyrone walked over with the redhead in tow. Bowing my head as he looked my way, Ty did the same, letting me move in peace. Feeling my nerves flood my head the closer I got to Shawty in the back, she stopped watching everybody else and eyed me. Almost like she knew I was coming to her, I walked past her, going to the wall near her chair, instead. Lighting a fresh blunt, her eyes sparked in my direction. Watching hungrily as I pulled the smoke inward, holding it as a thought swirled around my mind. *She smoke?* With my mouth still closed, I exhaled through my nose, watching *Miss Mary Mack's* tongue sliding slowly across her lips. *She does!*

Gaining a little more confidence with this thought, I kicked myself off the wall, stepping to her table and taking a seat. Silently blowing O's, Shawty couldn't keep her eyes off my blunt. *Ask me for it,* I challenged her with my eyes and watched her face flush red, before she turned away. Staring off at Ty, Travis, Torin, and the red-haired girl she came in with.

"Whatchu drinkin'?" I asked, snatching her cup from the tabled.

"Cranberry vodka sour."

Those were the three words, I thought as I inched the cup closer to my mouth. Pausing, I caught her watching me out the corner of my eye. Her left brow and the left corner of her mouth lifted, waiting on me to drink so she could get her glass back.

"You was just gon' let me boss yo shit?" I wondered, placing her glass back in front of her as she shrugged.

"*Oh,*" she giggled to herself as I turned, waiting to see what was so funny. "You were waiting on the—*Ew, I don't know where yo mouth been...* bit, *huh?*"

Laughing and nodding, she was right. It wasn't the smoothest of approaches but for a nigga like me, I rarely had to do much to get a bitch's attention. Taking her cup in her hands, Shawty downed her drink and raised it up before setting it back down.

"I'll tell you what..." she moved her body around so we were facing each other. "You can have this one coming, if I can have this right here," she slipped the blunt from behind my ear, placing it into her mouth without my permission.

Producing a lighter out of thin air, I watched her light my blunt and inhale. Mouth agape as she held the smoke better than a lot of niggas I know... She blew it out through her nose like I'd done while she was watching me. Chuckling just as a woman in a leotard came placing a fresh glass on the table, she looked to me as I shook my head, then sashayed away. I wasn't much of a drinker.

"*Wait*!" Shawty called out, stopping the bottle service girl before she got too far away from us. "Can you bring a bottle?"

"Of what?" Bottle-girl cocked her head to the side, eyeing me as I winked, getting her to blush.

"Just bring me vodka and a pitcher of orange juice and two glasses," Shawty in black turned to me smiling.

"Is that—"

"Yup!" Shawty tilted her head condescendingly as bottle-girl turned on her heels leaving.

"How you just gon' assume I'm finna drink witchu, Shawty?" I questioned her as I watched she continued smoking my blunt. "And gimme my shit back," I snatched it from her lips as she giggled.

"I just figured since you were picking up my glass that I could have something of yours," she narrowed her eyes at me and I could've sworn I say them sparkle. "And if you decide to sit with me, you have to drink—"

"Says who?" I countered, lowering my eyes to match her gaze as she giggled.

"Says me," she bit down on her bottom lip and I had to force myself to keep breathing.

"Wuss ya name?"

"*Carter...*"

Scrunching up my face in confusion, I didn't know if I heard her correctly so I opened my mouth to ask her again.

"*Carter!*" I heard my name a second time and shook my head, coming back to my bathroom. "Where were you?" Amani giggled as she clutched Dot in her arms, wrapped in a towel.

"*Damn,* I'on even know," I scratched the top of my head confused as Amani headed out the bathroom.

"You were just watching me," she explained as I sat on the edge of the bed. "You sure you're okay?"

"Yeah."

"You wanna talk about it?" She smirked causing me to smack my lips. "I'm just asking."

"You good..." I let her know I wasn't angry with her for checking on me. "We good."

"That we are," Amani inhaled, handing Dot over to me as she got her oiled down and pampered. "You're gonna put her to bed?" She asked after baby girl was in my arms.

"Yeah," I sighed as Dot's head fell into my chest. "*Eh,*" I tapped Amani as she crawled into bed. "Don't go to sleep."

"Okay," her face lit up.

"Freaky ass—"

"I was not even thinking about that," she flush red as I playfully shook my head.

"Nah, don't even try—"

"Carter, hush!" Amani giggled, pulling the covers over her body.

"You bet not go to sleep," I repeated as she yawned.

"I'm not, baby, I promise," she told me but I could see the over-glossed look in her eyes and knew if Dot fought me on getting in her crib, Amani would be out cold by the time I got back in our room.

Looking down at Dot, she was already gazing up on me. *Damn... I'm not getting none tonight.*

CHAPTER SEVEN

Amani

Back in my safe place, Dr. Clark gathered her notepad and pen and came over to her chair, across from where Carter and I were sitting. Pushing her block frames closer to her eyes, she jotted a few words down as I tried to read them upside down. With no luck, Dr. Clark lifted her pad up, crossing her legs and exhaled. *She was ready!*

"So, how are my favorite couple?" She asked as I beamed, looking over my shoulder at Carter who'd assume his usual, slouching back position on the loveseat.

"We're good?" I was still eyeing him as he shrugged then nodded.

"Why the uncertainty?" Dr. Clark addressed Carter as he cleared his throat, sitting up and clasping his hands together.

"It ain't no uncertainty," he assured her. "Everything's good."

"Great!" Dr. Clark showed her teeth as she wrote some more stuff down. "So no jokes before we begin?" She asked Carter as he dropped his head to laugh.

"Nah," he shook his head as he lifted it. "I know how to be serious durin' da appropriate times."

"It's okay to laugh in here," Dr. Clark urged as Carter looked to me then her. "This is a safe space," she moved her hands around to emphasize the point she was making.

"In dat case—" He paused to laugh, causing me and Dr. Clark to join him. "Nah, I ain't got nothin' right now, Doc... It's gotta be authentic," Carter stated as Dr. Clark's eyes widened.

"Oh, I see," she nodded her head, smirking. "I'll hold off on those then."

"*Oh,* please do," Carter boyishly countered as I giggled at him.

Flicking my chin, like he always did, I blushed as a direct result of it. Something only Carter seemed to be good at getting me to do. From the day I met him, he'd managed to keep me burning hot and chill at the same time. That was our vibe.

"Before I start, I wanna commend you both on your playful energy, not too many couples I've worked with have that... And it's a beautiful thing to witness," Dr. Clark stated as my eyes went to Carter's. "I can see your friendship in marriage and I'll tell you this—That will be the glue that holds your union together."

"Well, you know, I wasn't bout to wife nothin' but *goals,*" Carter swiped his thumb across his nose as he cockily shrugged. "Gotta set da example for da kids and in order to do dat..."

Carter rambled in jest while using his hands as he talked. "You gotta *be* da example—"

"Shut up!" I laughed while cutting him off, knowing he wouldn't stop talking until I did.

"There it is!" Dr. Clark chuckled as she scribbled a few things down. "Never lose that," she advised.

"We won't," I told her as Carter grabbed ahold of my hand, kissing the back of it.

"Alright... Let us begin," Dr. Clark sighed. "Amani, I'm going to shift gears a bit," she told me as I perked up on my cushion. "Let's talk about your mother—Jewel, *right*?"

At the mention of that name, a lump formed in my throat, clogging up my airways. During the first few session, Dr. Clark focused solely on my relationship with Carter. From the day we met, to getting married, up until now. She didn't even ask about our children. *So, how did she know about my mo— Carter!* Those damn papers he filled out the first day we came. That's how she knew about Jewel.

"Amani?"

"*Huh*?"

"Have you checked out, already?" Dr. Clark leaned forward in her chair as I looked over my shoulder at Carter, to see him staring back at me.

Shaking my head, I sat back to be closer to my husband as he instinctively tossed his arm over my shoulder. He was the only person I felt safe with enough to talk about my parents. Especially my mom but those conversations were still awkward, and they weren't frequent, either.

"No," I breathed, feeling Carter pulling me closer to him.

"Can you give me a little backstory on Jewel?" Dr. Clark already had her pen to the paper as I nodded my head. "How was your relationship as a child? Has it changed since growing up? Where is she now? All those things," Dr. Clark pitched her questions as I swallowed, realizing she didn't know what happened to Jewel.

"*Uh—She...*" I could feel my tongue swelling as the room got hotter.

Or maybe it wasn't but my palms were starting to sweat.

"She died," I stated flatly as Dr. Clark looked at me for more.

Looking over at Carter, he tilted his head for me to continue but I couldn't. I know I told him this before, but I never told him how she died.

"Amani?" Dr. Clark called my name again.

"She was murdered," I exhaled. "Stabbed forty-six times after her throat was sliced—Almost decapitating her."

"What?" Carter withdrew his hand from mine, taking his arm from around my neck as he sat up to look back at me. "You never told me dat."

"I know," my eyes danced around his face before dropping to my hands. "I don't tell anybody—I mean, most of the people who know me, back home, already know... Because it was on the news but *we* don't talk about it."

"*We*?" Dr. Clark spoke up as my eyes rose to look at her.

"My sisters—Salimah and Fatima."

"*Ah*, and you're the eldest?"

"Yeah," I nodded my head before dropping my eyes again.

Picking at the skin on my hands, I could feel it tingling after speaking on my mother's death. Something I've withheld from doing since I got the call, the day the police found her.

"If you don't mind me asking..." Dr. Clark got me to look at her. "Was her murder ever solved?"

Nodding my head, I could feel Carter burning holes through my side. I don't know if he was mad at me for not telling him or shocked but I didn't like this.

"Did you know the person who did it?"

“What kinda question is dat?” Carter cut in.

“An appropriate one considering the nature of the crime—”

“Crime of passion,” I interjected, nonchalantly. “And yeah... *She* was my mother’s girlfriend.”

The room was silent for a minute then Dr. Clark wrote incessantly. Filling an entire page and half of the back before she looked up from her notepad.

“My condolences to you and your sisters,” she sympathized before removing her block frames from her face.

“Thank you,” I was speaking to her but looking at Carter.

“What are you thinking, right now?” She asked.

“I don’t want you to be mad at me for not telling you this,” I told Carter as his face cinched.

“Why would I be mad, Shawty—Dats some traumatic ass shit, I wouldn’t expect you to be so open about but now I understand,” he told me while grabbing my hand, again.

“What do you understand, Carter?”

“How you feel—Or why you feel da way you do about Dot,” Carter told me as I exhaled. “From what you told me about da way she treated you and how she ran her house only to die like dat...” Carter blew out his breath is disbelief.

“If only I’d told you sooner?” I chimed in as Carter shook his head.

“No... But I’m glad I know now.”

Dropping my shoulders, there was relief but more remorse I hadn’t unleashed. Looking away from Carter, I figured this was the perfect time to live in my truth. Or own it.

“And now I want to be completely honest,” I rubbed my fingers together as my eyes dropped to my lap. “Jewel used to put us against each other—Mainly me and Salimah against Fatima,” I swallowed the lump that was trying to form in the back of my throat. “And she forced us to pick at her, fight her, and you know—Things like that... Then we got older and it became us." I turned towards Carter with tears in my eyes. "And if I didn't pick on Fatima then she'd come after me... And most of the time I didn't but I never stepped up to stop her or Salimah like a big sister should and *uh...*"

My chest felt heavy as I struggled to breathe properly. Taking small amounts of air through my nose, I fought to release them before bursting into tears.

"She didn't even do anything to me!" I cried. "And she was so little and innocent and I went along with—"

"It's not your fault—"

"But it is!" I cut Dr. Clark off. "I should've said something or tried to prevent it—I just accepted her fate and ultimately it got her kicked out then she met Torin..." I turned to Carter whose bleak expression pained me to see. "And that's why he hates us."

"Who's *Torin*?"

"My brother-in-law," I told Dr. Clark as she jotted more notes. "You've probably heard of him—The long-lost prince of Saudi Arabia," I revealed as her eyes widened with shock.

"*Really*?" She beamed as I nodded my head. "So, your baby sister is Fatima Rahim?"

"The one and only," I sighed.

"Oh, wow—That's right," she said to herself. "You're married so your—"

"Last name changed," I helped her finished the sentence. "Yeah..."

"And I read about her mother's murder a few years back but I didn't even think to put two-and-two together," Dr. Clark told me as I continued nodding my head. "*Wow*—Alright, coming back into this session," Dr. Clark circled her arms around the air as she breathed. "There's a lot of childhood trauma and repressed memories and victim-blaming because you, Amani, were a victim, as well." She told me as I twisted my lips. "So, you can't hold yourself accountable, especially not the child you were. I can't even begin to imagine the amount of stress you endured while choosing between your sister and your mother. It's traumatic—That's the best word to describe it."

Looking to Carter, his face hadn't changed, and that worried me. Maybe my honesty struck a chord in him. One where he realized I wasn't the angelic, goodie-girl type he fell for and probably planned on leaving me.

"Mr. Banks... You still there?" Dr. Clark did what I wanted to do.

Bringing Carter into the conversation.

"Yeah."

"How you feeling?" She asked as he jerked his shoulders. "Can I have a word or two on the subject?"

"Shock."

"From what?" Dr. Clark was pulling teeth.

"Everything, man..." Carter sighed as he caught my gaze and immediately turned away.

Feeling low, my head dropped in shame. *He was going to leave me,* I thought as tears filled my eyes.

"I thought I knew my wife but I don't—"

"Why are you crying?" Dr. Clark cut him off to address me.

"Because he's gonna leave me," I whimpered, looking up at her.

"What—Mani, I ain't gon'—"

Beep. Beep. Beep.

The session was over. Just as I was having my breakthrough, we were done. Sniffling as I accepted the Kleenex from Dr. Clark, I dabbed my eyes then blew my nose.

"Aw, man, if I didn't have a two o'clock I'd extend this session," Dr. Clark groaned while looking at the watch on her right arm. "I'll tell you what—I have a homework assignment for you both," she stated as Carter pulled me into him, kissing the top of my head. "I want you to focus on what drew you to each other and what locked you in—Meaning, the first time you laid eyes on one another, what was it that intrigued you? And when was the moment that you realized you could spend the rest of your lives together?"

"So, what—Do we do what we used to do when we first met and started dating?" Carter asked as Dr. Smith smiled.

"Exactly—Do what you used to do when you first started dating... That means movie dates, dinner, whatever it was you did during the wooing stage of your relationship," she explained. "And when you come back, next week, we can work on the parenting part of your relationship."

Swallowing, as I lifted my head from Carter's chest, I wasn't looking forward to next week. This Jewel episode got a little too real for my liking.

"I'll see you next week," Dr. Clark stood up with her hand extended, like she did every time our sessions ended. "And you remember what I said... None of what your mother did to you or made you do is your fault—Even though Fatima was used as the scapegoat... Mental and emotional abuse is still abuse."

"Okay," was all I could say as I shook Dr. Clark's hand and stepped to the side so that Carter could do the same.

Leaving the clinic with a different feeling than I'd came in with spoke volumes to what Carter tried explaining on the day he brought me in. He right to bring me here. Dr. Clark understood me and she was the perfect medium to all my problems. The catalyst for renewed life or a stress-free one.

"You want somethin' to eat?" Carter asked as he helped me into his truck. "You sure?" He said when I shook my head, declining his offer.

"Yeah," I exhaled, clicking my seatbelt on. "I'll just make a sandwich or something, when we get home," I told him as he nodded, closing my door.

"I'll just take us home and we'll get the kids later," he told me while starting up the truck.

And I didn't disagree because I needed to sleep this off and afterwards, take a shower, too.

PULLING into our driveway as Carter hit the button to the lift, I couldn't wait, so I popped my seatbelt off. Feeling a hand on my thigh, I looked over to see Carter shaking his head. My chest tightened with worry as I waited for him to pull through the garage and park.

"Lemme ask you somethin'," he finally spoke to me after the long, quiet drive home. "You still smoke?"

Throwing my head back laughing, I knew he was serious but his question wasn't any less funny to me. Especially after the session we'd just had, I'd expect him to ask anything but this. Plus, he knew I hadn't indulged since I found out I was pregnant with Dot... But I knew what he meant by asking me.

"Yeah, I do."

"Why you don't come blow with me like you used to?" He asked as my shoulders rose and fell.

I hadn't really thought about it much to put a reason to it. Between stressing over school and being homesick while mulling over why I couldn't connect with my daughter—Picking up a blunt seemed trivial. Actually, it hadn't crossed my mind, really. And that's saying a lot because there was a time I couldn't wake without baking.

"You wanna hotbox da whip?" The corners of his mouth curled up as he lifted the armrest.

Staring inside the compartment, Carter had stacks of rolling woods and grinders. He usually did his smoking inside his truck so it was no surprise that he was prepared for an impromptu steam in the garage. Dropping the sun visor down, two blunts fell into his lap as I giggled and shook my head. Watching him pick up one and light it, Carter extended the blunt towards me and I grabbed it. Staring at the slow burning wood while taking in its funky aroma... I was reluctant at first. *Do what you used to do when you first started dating...* I heard and thought, *what of it.*

Inhaling slowly, I couldn't stop the smile spreading across my face. *It's been too long, old friend,* I thought as I took another pull. Savoring the moment, I held in enough smoke for the both of us. Ignoring the circle rules, *puff, puff, give...* The blunt was already gone before I realized I never passed it.

"Sorry," I giggled as Carter shrugged it off.

"Look atchu," he grinned, flicking my chin.

My eyes were low and I could tell the difference. I felt loopy, like the first time I ever hit a bowl. It was overwhelmingly satisfying. *Abstinence makes the heart beat faster....* Oh, wait, I think you can only use that word for sex.

"Yo ass faded," Carter laughed at me as I tried to stop smiling.

"Do you think this is gonna mess with my therapy?" I asked him, remembering the downside of getting high.

During the first blunt, I enjoyed blissful heights but my mind also released my darkest, repressed memories. The ones I bottled up to keep from haunting me during my daily routines.

"Nah..." Carter shook his head as he lit another blunt,

handing it to me. "We doin' what we used to do," he laughed with me. "But dats why we're doin' dis shit right now," he said as my neck snapped in his direction.

"What do you mean?" I asked with the blunt touching my lips, worrying that the next words coming out his of mouth would ruin the whole hotbox.

"So you can sleep it off."

Thinking for a second, I mulled over his logic, nodded then inhaled. *Makes sense to me.* Enjoying my second blunt, Carter lit a third and indulged himself. Like old times, I'd forgotten how good it felt to smoke some good weed. And for a brief moment, Brandon came to mind. He was the reason I turned into a burnout. The fun times we used to have after school, blowing in the alley behind his aunt Afiwa's house. Then his cousin, Geante would catch us and supply our growing habit with intentions of getting us to sell. Something I refused but not Brandon. He saw this opportunity as a way to fund his life and became my go-to supplier, after that.

Taking a deep breath as I lowered the blunt, those happy memories faded. No matter how good it was, sitting beside Carter only reminded me that *all good things end.* And my best friend became public enemy number one, to me. Swallowing as the events that led up to me meeting Carter swirled around in my head, I smiled as I pictured us in Brunner's. At that back table behind all the action. To think, a couple blunts and a pitcher of screwdriver would grant me my twin flame. *It was all surreal at one point.*

Looking to my left as Carter held out another blunt, I gabbed it, ashing the second. Putting it to my lips and inhaling a wilder thought came to mind. Grinning as smoke blew from my nose, I climbed on my feet so I was crouching in the seat.

"Whatchu do—" Carter couldn't even finish questioning me as I crawled into his lap.

Squished between his body and the steering wheel, I wrapped my arms around his neck gazing into his bright green eyes. With the blunt still dangling from my lips, Carter reached for it just as he moved his seat back. Instant relief could be felt as the tension on my chest and back subsided. Plopping the blunt between his lips, I watched hungrily as the smoke escaped his parted mouth and nostrils like steam from a hot pot.

Already high, this new hankering I had was sexual. Almost insatiable, but I knew how to quench it. Diving face first into the side of his neck, I could feel his hands already caressing my backside as I kissed and sucked. Regressing to my younger days, I left passion marks all along his neckline, just for fun.

"Quit doin' dat shit," Carter squeezed my right cheek as he caught on to what I was doing, after the fourth one.

"*Why?* You can do it to me," I offered as he pulled me away from his neck.

"I'ma do a lil moe than dat—C'mon," he hit the locks on his door as I quickly grabbed his hand. "Whatchu doin'?"

"I wanna do it in here," I told him as his eyes shifted down my body.

Folding his bottom lip into his mouth, I could see him thinking. With the blunt between his fingers, Carter placed it in my mouth then hiked my dress up. *I guess he's game!*

CHAPTER EIGHT

Carter

Down the street from Dede's complex, Dot was giving me and her brother the blues. Crying from the moment I put her into the car seat, she was working on a new record.

"C'mon, lil Shawty—We here!" I tried consoling her from the front, but it wasn't working.

"Do she got her pacifier?" Cairo questioned me as I nodded. "Her gums must really be hurtin' then," he stated as I pulled into an empty space near the mailboxes.

"Nah, I'on think so," I told him, remembering how I rubbed Orajel on her gums after she ate to ease the pain. "She just don't like dat seat."

"You better get used to it, Dot!" Cairo called out to his sister before he opened his door to leave.

Turning with one leg dangling out the door, Cairo threw his arms around me then pulled back to shake up. Something he'd been doing since he was a toddler.

"See, ya later boy," I pulled him into another hug, kissing the top of his head before he grabbed his bag and got out.

Going to the back door, he opened it and climbed in next to Dot's car seat. Stopping her loud cries, she was still whimpering, but having her brother near her calmed her down.

"Bye Dot."

I looked over my shoulder as Cairo leaned in to kiss his sister. Grabbing at his head, Dot got a handful of his hair in her hands and pulled.

"Ahhh, lemme go!" Cairo yelled as Dot's screaming kicked back up. "Daddy!" He called out to me for help as I chuckled, grabbing ahold of Dot's hand and working her finger loose so Cairo could leave. "Dang, Dot—It's like dat?" Cairo fluffed the top of his head as I continued laughing at him. "I see y'all next week."

Watching Cairo walk to his mama's door, he knocked and seconds later Dede opened it for him. Scooting to the side, Cairo squeezed between her and disappeared. Using this as my cue, I caught Dede waving to me as she held her finger up to hold me off while she poked her head into her house. Walking over to my truck, I let the window down, knowing she could hear Dot's cries.

"Hey—*Awww*," she giggled as she got to the window. "She is not happy in that seat."

"At all," I agreed.

"So, I kinda need a favor from you."

"What is it?"

Opening her mouth, Dede stopped, then closed it. She was trying to figure out the best way to ask me.

"I've been dating this guy for six months now and things are getting serious between us," she told me as I nodded once. "And I know how you feel about me bringing niggas around—"

"Cairo, so you want me to meet em?" I finished her sentence as she cracked a smile, nodding. "When?"

"*Umm*, I was thinking this weekend—Or whenever you're not busy."

"A'ight," I started to say yes, but then I remembered what I had planned for Amani this Saturday. "I'll hitchu up—Prolly won't be dis weekend but Monday or Wednesday for sho," I told Dede as she smiled the entire time. "You really like dis dude, *huh*?"

"Yeah, I do," she gushed, clasping her hands together. "He might be the one!" she crossed her fingers in high hopes.

"*Eh*, I'm rootin' for you, Shawty—He just gotta pass da Carter test."

"Boy, stop!" Dede laughed with me as she playfully shoved me. "If he passes your test or not, you're just meeting him for Cairo," Dede played annoyed as she rolled her eyes. "Hey, she stopped crying!" She pointed out Dot's silence as I looked behind me to the mirror attached to her car seat.

I could see Dot's eyes, bright and open, as she lied still, listening to my conversation. *Nosey self!*

"Nah, she just heard yo ass and she know you ain't her mama," I laughed with Dede. "You finna get me in trouble—*I heard my daddy talkin' to—*"

"You so stupid!" Dede nudged my shoulder, laughing. "Well, lemme get outta here, then."

"A'ight, Shawty!" I waited until she backed away from my truck to roll the window up.

Looking over my shoulder to view the car seat mirror, before I backed out only to see Dot's eyes, now closed. I chuckled softly and drove off. *Allat cryin' and carryin' out just to go right to sleep.*

Racing on the highway, I was on a mission to make it to my parents' house before the USPS courier delivered their mail. I had some shit coming in and I didn't want my mama doing her usual snoop act and opening my mail up before I got ahold of it.

With a quarter till twelve, I made perfect timing. Turning into their driveway, I looked over my shoulder just as I popped off my seatbelt. Lil Shawty was still knocked out as I cheered silently. Careful not to slam my door after I got out, I quietly opened the backdoor, unhooking Dot's seat and grabbing her bag.

Careful not to shake the car seat too much as I walked into my parents' house, my mama was coming down the steps as I put my finger to my lips. Smiling and nodding her head, she pointed up the steps.

"You can put her in our bed," she whispered as I nodded, following her directions up to the master bedroom.

Unbuckling Dot and removing her from the seat, she sighed in her sleep as I smiled down at her. *Yeah, you free lil Shawty.* Checking her forehead, she was already sweating as I removed her pants, shoes and socks. Stacking the surrounding pillows. Once I was sure she was secure, I left.

"How you doin' mama," I kissed her cheek as I came into the kitchen.

"I'm doing just fine, Bubba—How's my daughter?" She asked me as I looked over my shoulder to see my father coming into the kitchen.

"Hey," he tapped my shoulder before going into the fridge.

"Wussup, Daddy," I spoke then turned my attention back to my mama. "She doin' better—School is finished so now I'm just lookin' forward to da *you know what,*" I winked at my mama as she giggled.

"Oh, you and me both—Which reminds me," my mama gushed as she turned to the drawer behind her bringing out a manilla folder. "What do you think about these?"

Glossing over the color schemes and patterns, I already knew which ones weren't making the cut. Yellow was out, pink, orange, and red. Scrunching up my face as my mama's smile faded, she knew I wasn't feeling none of this shit.

"You don't like—"

"Hell nah!" I scoffed as my Pop's chuckled.

"Okay, so what about—"

"I want somethin' subtle, mama—Not dis flamboyant shit you love pickin' out," I told her as her mouth fell open. "Think light—Issa lite affair and Mani already don't like a crowd," I told her as she sighed heavily.

"Sounds to me like you should be doin' the plannin' then," my Pop's added as I scratched the side of my face.

"You might be right—"

"Oh, don't gang up on me!" My mama scolded me and my father as we laughed at her. "This ain't my first go-round," she rolled her eyes as the grin on my face grew.

"So, make it happen, captain!"

"*Hush,* Bubba—"

DING. DONG.

Jumping up, I already knew it was for me. Hearing my parents laughing, I smirked as I opened the front door. *Right on time!*

"Hi, Carter Banks?" The mail lady was snickering as I took the signing pad from her hand. "Thank you—"

"No, thank you!"

"Oh, wow—Whatever you got that's making you this pleasant... I need it for my entire route!" she giggled while placing the four boxes in my hand.

"It's food," I told her and watched her eyes gleam. "You know it's da way to most people's heart!"

"Don't I know it," she rubbed her stomach then turned away. "You have a great rest of your day."

"I will!"

Closing the door and going back into the kitchen, both of my parents were gone. My mama was probably checking on Dot and my Pop's probably couldn't wait to get back to the den. It didn't matter because I was leaving soon, anyway. Going into my mama's crafting closet, she always kept gift bags and wrapping paper for birthdays and special occasions. Valentine's Day, Easter bunnies, shamrocks, Santa and everything in between... I thought for a second then grabbed the golden, "Good tidings" wrap. Not even close to Christmas. This wrapping paper still held greater sentimental value.

Taking it into the kitchen, I got to work on the four boxes. Not to brag, but my gift wrapping skills could rival a department store clerk's. Ask Cairo.

"What are you doing—*Christmas*?" My mama came in after I'd taped up the last package.

"Yeah," I grinned as I held the package up. "I got somethin' special planned—Whatchu doin' up?" I frown at Dot as she reached out for me.

Her face was beet red, and I knew she'd been upstairs crying while I was retrieving my packages. *Her ass don't ever wanna sleep.*

"Daddy bout to go, lil Shawty," I told her while kissing her forehead. "You gon' have to take a real nap."

"Oh, she will," my mama promised as she prepped a fresh bottle. "That's why they key to getting her to stay asleep is to nap with her—"

"I can't do dat—"

"And that's why she doesn't stay sleep."

"She gon' learn today!" I teased, kissing my baby girl again before placing her in my mama's arms. "Eh, but I think I know how I'ma set up da theme." I told my mama as she fed Dot.

"And the colors, too?"

"Yeah, mint—I'ma email Mindy Schultz," I told my mama as I scooped my packages up. "You gon' love it!"

"I better after the way you tossed mine out the window!"

"It was for good reason—"

"Hush up, Bubba," she told me as we laughed. "You can leave her today—"

"Who you tryna show my baby off to?" I called her out as the corners of her mouth curled up.

"Jilly's coming to town and I want her to meet my red-hair baby doll!" My mama gushed as Dot popped her bottle from her mouth.

Laughing at her reaction, I nodded, then shrugged. It actually worked in my favor. I'd have a full day for me and my wife... As the doctor prescribed. And we could do more than just smoke and fuck. *Even if I loved doing both with her*.

"A'ight, cool—I'll see y'all later," I hugged and kissed my mama, then kissed my baby girl and I was out.

"Hey, mama," I popped in on Amani as she lounged in the living room channel surfing.

Lifting her head over the couch, she was smiling already. Holding the packages behind my back, it didn't take Amani long to suspect something was going.

"What are you hiding?" She asked while crawling to her knees.

Raising my shoulders as I looked off to the side, Amani's soft giggling put a smile on my face.

"Carter—"

"Amani."

"Can you show me?" She begged as I shook my head. "So, why did you even bring it in here for me to see?"

"You can't see shit cuz they behind my back—"

"But I know they're there and that was your point," she cut her eyes at me as my shoulders rose slowly. "You gon' show me what you're hiding!" Amani swiftly jumped over the couch, running over to me as I shifted to the right, causing her to slip and fall.

Laughing as she sat on her ass pouting, I pulled the boxes from behind me. Watching her sour face sweeten, I extended my arm out to help her up.

"I was gon' show you anyway—"

"Shut up," Amani rolled her eyes as I chuckled while handing her the first box.

"Let's take it to da kitchen," I suggested as Amani tore through the wrapping paper. "C'mon," I urged as she thought too long on it.

Following behind me, I placed the rest of the boxes on the countertop, going into one of the drawers for a butter knife. Handing it to Amani, she opened the first box and giggled when she read the gift card.

"Carter," she gushed while sliding the knife through the packing tape to pop open the box. "*Oou,* and I was just craving dipped Italian beef with sweet and hot peppers, too!" She stared at the Portillo's kit with a goofy smile plastered on her face.

"There's more," I told her as I handed off the second box.

"And I love the Christmas paper," she gleamed.

"I knew you would," I puffed my chest out, cockily as she giggled.

Eager to get this one open, Amani didn't waste any time tearing through the wrapping paper. Laughing as she saw the next gift, a couple deep dish pizzas from Giordano's.

"You know what's funny?" she looked over at me as I shook my head. "I actually want these," she giggled by herself as my face scrunched up in confusion.

"Whatchu mean?"

"Real Chicagoans don't care about Giordano's—I mean, they're good but when we want pizza, this ain't the place we call up," she explained to me as I nodded slowly. "But since I've been away... I'll take it!"

"You better," I teased as she twisted her lips, impatiently waiting for the next two boxes.

"Gimme more!" she demanded as I took a step back, sliding the gifts with me.

"Who you talkin' to—"

"Carter!"

"Nah," I shook my head as she groaned and giggled. "You, Dot and Ro seem to have shit twisted—Y'all not gon' talk to me any kinda way and expect me to reward y'all!" I ranted as she crossed her arms over her chest. "A'ight, bet," I nodded once, sliding the two presents off the countertop as she quickly unfolded her arms, laughing. "Nah, don't try to come correct, now—"

"Okay, okay, I'm sorry!" Amani followed me out the kitchen, grabbing my shirt as my right foot touched the first step. "Carter!"

Ignoring her all the way up the stairs, down the hall and into our bedroom, I didn't stop until I was in my closet. Amani still had my shirt balled up in her fists as I placed the boxes on the jewelry case.

"You not gettin' deez today," I told her as she poked her lip out, pouting.

"*Then you won't get none from me tonight,*" she mumbled underneath her breath, but I heard her.

Turning around, I caught Amani off guard, snatching her up and twirling her into me. Lost for words, she giggled as I shook my head, gazing down into her face.

"Whatchu say?"

"I didn't say anything," she lied as I cut my eyes at her.

"You gon' gimme some cuz it's mine," I stated as she gasped then giggled.

"It's yours?" Amani batted her eyes as I leaned in closer to her face.

"Whose is it, then?"

"Mine," she grinned seductively.

Licking my lips as I gazed into her eyes, she fought for as long as she could, but the minute my lips touched hers, Amani melted in my arms. Talking big shit and can never back it up.

"You know dat pussy got my name written on it," I pulled her into me, squeezing her ass as she squealed. "*Ah—Oou, Carter, wait... UHH—Oou, okay, okay, Mmm,*" I mimicked her love sounds as her eyes bucked in embarrassment.

"You think you're so funny," Amani smirked as I nodded my head up and down. "Why can't I have my last two gifts tonight?" She whined as I shook my head. "Why not?"

"Who said they was for you?"

"You did," she retorted as I exhaled, then shrugged. "*Pleaseeee*? With a cherry on top!"

Pecking her lips as she begged me, I started walking us out

of my closet. With Amani still wrapped in my arms, she tried to wiggle free, but she couldn't. Making it over to the bed, I let her loose, digging into my pocket for my phone.

"I'll give it to you when it's time," I told her as she exhaled deeply, causing me to laugh. "Mani, just relax—It'll mean more given in da context, in which, it's intended," I told her as she slowly sat up on the bed. "What?" I asked after a smile appeared on her face.

"You're learning!"

"Bout what?"

"You didn't curse—"

"It'll mean more given in da *fuckin'* context, in which it's *muthafuckin'* intended—*Shit*," I smirked as her smiled flipped upside down. "You shoulda neva brought it up—"

"It's such a shame," Amani sighed, rolling her eyes to the side as I lowered my head to level with hers.

"No, what's a shame is you tryna change how I am—Mani, you gotta love every part of me, Shawty," I pecked her lips as she threw her arms around my neck.

"I do love every part of you," she told me as I smacked my lips, not buying it. "I do!"

"Tell me anything, Shawty," I stood up with Amani still linked to me.

Lifting her up, I had a flashback of the day after we first met. When I had her up against the wall, calling my name. It was that day, after the bullshit she tried pulling, that I realized there was more to her... And I needed more time with her to find out. Squeezing her ass as she giggled into my ear, *it's grub time!*

"C'mon, let's put dat food on!"

Not waiting on a response, I ran with Amani screaming in my arms, all the way down the steps. Not stopping until we were in the kitchen. Plopping her on the countertop, she sat there, talking to me as I did most of the work. Not that I mind doing anything for her. That's my baby, and that's what I'm here for. *Lighten every load.* For the rest of our lives.

CHAPTER NINE

Amani

Flipping through channels, I wasn't interested in anything showing right now. There was nothing good on besides reruns I'd seen and probably end up re-watching. Sighing and twisting my lips, I stopped at **MTV2**. My Wife and Kids was on, and I'd always liked this show growing up. *At least I'd laugh,* I thought while setting the remote on the coffee-table.

Throwing my arms behind my head, I tried to get comfortable and rest, but I couldn't. Something was ailing me. And it wasn't being alone, again. Actually, I'd grown to love my temporary solitude. It gave me a chance to miss my family... Not, saying I didn't but you know the saying. *Absence makes the heart grow fonder.*

Sitting up, again, my eyes shifted to the left of the coffee table where my laptop was lying. Feeling my heartbeat quicken, the answer to my uneasiness lied in my emails. The one I'd been ignoring and putting off for a few weeks, now. Running my tongue over my top teeth as I internally weighed my options, curiosity got the best of me. Dodging forward, I opened and unlocked my laptop and went straight to the internet. *Google IS NOT your friend, girl... Don't do it!*

Ignoring my own warnings as I lied back on the armrest of the couch, I typed in BJ's full name. *Brandon Kosi Jennings.* Allowing the page to populate, I could see pictures of Brandon accepting awards and speaking at seminars. Something he'd always done, but it looked to be more frequent or he changed clothes every hour. Either way, he was doing good—Making a name for himself outside of Chicago and I was proud of that. Scrolling through Google, I stopped on a photo of him and a woman I'd never seen before. She was cute. Nothing like the dusty females he stayed bringing to his apartment to smash. She looked classy and astute and I knew she was on a similar intellectual caliber as Brandon. Clicking on their image, more pictures of them popped up. BJ was holding her close with his arm wrapped around her lower waist, in one pic and the one I saw after that one showed him kissing her.

Staring at the two of them, I felt a twinge of anger. Not from jealousy, but just from the fact that Brandon still reached out to me while having this woman on his arm. Further proving how little he felt of me or my feelings... *If I had any left for him.* Clicking on the pictures to view the date, I scoffed and shook my head. *He'll never change,* I thought to myself. I guess that's what I get for mulling over his pointless email. *I should've deleted it the moment my phone pinged.*

"Hey, mama!" I heard Carter as I shook a little from the shock of him popping up on me.

Quickly slamming my laptop closed, I peered over the couch, smiling. *Fuck Brandon,* I thought as I took in my man's beauty. And Carter was a vision to the gods. Slim cut with muscles in all the right places. *My beige, pink-lipped Romeo—With eyes like clovers...* I truly was a lucky girl.

"What are you hiding?" I asked him as I noticed his arms behind his back.

Lifting his shoulders and looking off to the side, I giggled at his silliness.

"Carter—"

"Amani!" He cut me off just to childishly mock me.

"Can you show me?" I whined as he shook his head, causing my shoulders to drop. "So, why did you even bring it in here for me to see?"

"You can't see shit cuz they behind my back—"

"But I know they're there and that was your point," I narrowed my eyes in his direction as he laughed. "You gon' show me what you're hiding!" I demanded as I sprung my body over the couch to run up on him.

Side swiping my attempt, I ended up slipping and falling on my butt. Hearing Carter's laughs only made me madder as I crossed my arms over my chest, poking my lip out. It took him a minute to stop laughing as he revealed the four gifts he was hiding from me. Turning my frown upside down as I grabbed his hand to help me on my feet, Carter handed me the top box. Excited was an understatement, as I poked a hole in the festive wrapping paper.

"I was gon' show you anyway—"

"Shut up," I playfully groaned as he smirked.

"Let's take it to da kitchen," Carter suggested, but I was

already halfway through the wrapper to care. "C'mon," he hooked his hand to my arm and pulled me along.

Tailing him to the kitchen, Carter plopped the other three boxes on the counter as he let me go, going into the silverware drawer to retrieve a butter knife. Giving it to me, as I read his gift card, I cut the packing tape and giggled.

"Carter!" I cooed as I pulled the meal kit from the box. "*Oou,* and I was just craving dipped Italian beef with sweet and hot peppers, too!"

"There's more," he told me while handing off the second box.

Giggling at the Christmas theme he went with, I felt giddy already and I hadn't even opened this next gift.

"And I love the Christmas paper," I beamed as his face lit up.

"I knew you would." His chest raised as I sniggled.

Just as I did with the first gift, it didn't take but a second to get this one opened. Laughing as I read off the top, I could already feel my mouth watering in anticipation.

"You know what's funny?" I giggled while looking over at Carter as he shook his head. "I actually want these," I kept laughing even after his face curled in confusion.

"Whatchu mean?"

I could detect the offense in his tone as I softened my face and stopped laughing, altogether. *Oops, I better reel it back in.*

"Real Chicagoans don't care about Giordano's—I mean, they're good but when we want pizza, this ain't the place we call up," I told him, hoping my wording didn't crush the romance he'd clearly thought long and hard about. "But since I've been away... I'll take it!" My smile sealed the deal as I watched Carter mimic it.

"You better," he grinned as my eyes shifted to the last two gifts.

"Gimme more!" I demanded after he took too long for my liking.

"Who you talkin' to—"

"Carter!" I wasn't in the mood for waiting any longer.

"Nah," his smile quickly faded as I giggled. "You, Dot and Ro seem to have shit twisted—Y'all not gon' talk to me any kinda way and expect me to reward y'all!" he ranted as I exhaled, crossing my arms over my chest like he was annoying me. "A'ight bet!" He nodded while sliding the two last gifts from the counter as my arms fell. "Nah, don't try to come correct now—"

"Okay, okay, I'm sorry!" I pleaded as Carter continued out the kitchen. "Carter!"

Grabbing for him, I snagged his shirt as he stomped up the steps. Ignoring my apology and pleas for him to forgive me, Carter stomped his way into our bedroom and his closet, where he sat the two gifts on his jewelry counter.

"You not gettin' deez today," he told me as I frowned.

"*Then you won't get none from me tonight,*" I mumbled underneath my breath.

Thinking he didn't hear me, Carter turned too quickly for me to react as he yanked me into his arms. Sighing, I didn't have words as his emerald eyes bore into mine.

"Whatchu say?" His cool breath tickled my lips as I bit down on my bottom.

"I didn't say anything," I lied, and I knew he knew it, too, by the way his eyes narrowed.

"You gon' gimme some cuz it's mine," he growled into my face as I sighed and giggled.

"It's yours?" I could feel my temperature rising as Carter's left brow rose.

"Whose is it, then?" He beckoned as I took this opportunity to really heat things up.

"Mine," I grinned to emphasize where I was going with this banter.

Eyeing me like his favorite bowl of cereal, I counted down internally, knowing that any minute he'd be all over me. Licking his lips just as his face inched closer to mine, Carter paused just before his forehead touched mine as I stopped breathing. Pressing his lips to mine, I exhaled. Feeling my chest cave in as he tongued me down.

"You know dat pussy got my name written on it," he roared, grabbing my butt and squeezing it as I giggled. "*Ah—Oou, Carter, wait... UHH—Oou, okay, okay, Mmm...*"

My face burned as the fluttery sensations in my chest quickened. I know he thought I was a prude, but I enjoyed knowing he listened to my love cries. Only Carter could get me to that point, and I hope he knew how well he laid the pipe.

"You think you're so funny," I grinned as Carter nodded his head up and down. "Why can't I have my last two gifts tonight?" I kept at it as he shook his head. "Why not?"

"Who said they was for you?"

"You did," I answered quickly as he sighed and shrugged. "*Pleaseeee*? With a cherry on top!" I begged him, hoping he'd cut the shenanigans and just give me my gifts.

Pecking my lips, instead, Carter walked us out of his closet, keeping me locked in his arms. Squirming, trying to break free, there was no use. He overpowered me every time and now was no different. Flinging me onto the bed, I did the only thing I could do. Pouting with my arms crossed, Carter laughed at me.

"I'll give it to you when it's time," he told me as he peered down at his phone before looking back up at me. "Mani, relax—It'll mean more given in da context, in which, it's intended," he stated as the right corner of my mouth turned up. "What?"

"You're learning," I grinned because he was clueless.

"Bout what?"

"You didn't curse—"

"It'll mean more given in da *fuckin'* context, in which it's *muthafuckin'* intended—*Shit*," Carter cut me off, doing the very thing I disliked, as he boyishly laughed. "You shoulda neva brought it up—"

"It's such a shame," I blew out a breath, rolling my eyes as Carter bent down to look in my face.

"No, what's a shame is you tryna change how I am," he countered as I giggled. "Mani, you gotta love every part of me, Shawty," he pecked my lips as I threw my arms around his neck.

Despite his foul mouth, nothing could get me out of the mood he'd put me in. Tonight was going to end in bliss. *Sweet sexual bliss.*

"I do love every part of you," I cooed as he smacked his lips. "I do!"

"Tell me anything, Shawty," he stood up, pulling me along with him.

Wrapping my legs around his waist, I watched Carter lose himself in my eyes and wondered what he thought about when he disappeared in the moment. Whatever it was had him bulging out of his pants and I was ready to pounce on it.

"C'mon, let's put dat food on!" He came to as I blinked, feeling him grip me tighter before taking off.

Squealing and laughing, Carter ran like Cairo, down the stairs, jumping two steps from the bottom, too. Bouncing and shaking me, I didn't stop laughing until he sat me up top of the counter.

"You play too much," I told him as he started opening the packaging and preparing my food.

Turning on the oven, he spun around towards me, grinning.

"You love it," he told me something I already knew. "Yeah, you do," Carter flicked my chin as he stood between my legs.

Palming the counter to keep him balanced, I slipped him some tongue, still trying to kick things off as he laughed in the middle of it. Hugging him underneath his arms, I pulled Carter into me.

"You gon' hold me here—"

"Yup," I cut him off as he dropped his face into the crook of my neck to laugh.

"And then what?" He asked as he pulled back.

"Make you do stuff with me," my voice was low and sensual as Carter's snickering came to an end.

"Do what stuff?" He talked against my lips.

"Fun stuff," I grinned with him.

"What's fun—What we do dats fun?" He was playing my game.

"*Mmm*... Like," I looked upwards as I fantasized about past love making.

I could name a million things right now, but they'd only drive me crazy.

"You ain't tell me," he pushed my buttons as I grinned, gazing back into his eyes.

"Kissing," came out of my mouth in one hushed breath.

"Like dis?" Carter gave me the juiciest kiss as I shivered. "Now what?"

"*Uhh*," I tried to contain my hormones the hotter I got.

My only saving grace was us being fully dressed.

"Touching," I swallowed as Carter picked up his right hand, placing it on my upper thigh and squeezing.

"Touching what?" His eyes never left mine as his hand moved down between the groove then back up. "Tell me whatchu want me to touch," he spoke softly against my lips when I didn't answer back.

"*Umm*," I panted as my chest heaved up and down. "*Tuh*—Touch *it*," I stuttered as his fingers pulled the waistband of my shorts, giving him enough room to slide his hand through.

"Touch it?" He asked me as he did the same with my panties, feeling the tip of his finger on my pearl.

Massaging my clit, I closed my eyes immediately, knowing that if we kept looking at each other, I'd cum.

"Nah, look at me," Carter demanded as my eyes cinched even tighter. "Mani," he called me, speeding up the tempo as my eyes shot open. "Tell me whatchu want."

"I want it..."

"Whatchu want?" His voice became gruff, the closer he got me to ecstasy.

"I want it—*Oou*," I moaned as soon as he slid his finger into me.

"You want it?" He asked, rubbing his thumb against my clit as he worked his finger inside me.

"Yeah," I panted with my mouth open.

"Then say it."

"Say what?" I was doing all my breathing through my mouth the more aroused I became.

"Whose is it?"

He brought it back to earlier when I claimed *it* as mine. Gasping as I laughed once again, he got me. My laughing only lasted a second, though, as he hit a wall, breaking my levee.

"Whose is it?" He whispered against my lips as I squeezed my thigh muscles, trying to get him to take his hands from between my legs.

"*Oou—Okay*," my chest heaved as I trembled.

"Okay, who?"

"*Sss—You!*" I grabbed at his hand as he inserted another finger.

"*You, who?*" He was playing a dangerous game with my nerves, as I squirmed from the feeling he was giving me.

"*Carter—Oh my God!*" I erupted right on the countertop with Carter standing between my legs. "It's yours..." I finally breathed as he stopped applying pressure.

Pecking my lips as he pulled his hand back, Carter did what he always did when he had his fingers inside of me. Sucking them clean as I watched with my bottom lip tucked into my mouth.

BEEP!

The oven dinged as I flinched before laughing.

"Scary ass," Carter chuckled. "And quit usin' God's name in vain," he flicked my chin as I giggled.

"I forgot about the food—"

"Fuck dat food—I'm finna eat you," I talked over me while grabbing ahold of my ankles so I'd fall back.

"On the counter?" I gasped with my legs sprawled out.

"Where else I'm supposed to eat?" He asked me as my eyes wandered off to the side, unintentionally. "Da dinin' room—"

"No!" I giggled as he lifted me up from the countertop.

"It's mine, right?" He asked as he carried me, bridal style, into the dining room. "So, I can have it where I want it."

Technically, he was right. And I really wanted it, so I couldn't fight him on where it took place. *It is what it is...*

CHAPTER TEN

Carter

Kicking my feet up on the coffee table, today was probably the only day I had to myself, in a long time. Usually, I was out running errands or cleaning up behind my cousin and brother or dropping my kids off with my parents. Keeping the peace and making sure everybody's shit balances out before my own. But today, I was gonna roll my blunt and smoke them in the crib like the king of the castle should—

DING. DONG.

Sitting completely still, I knew whoever was at the door

would ring the bell again so my dolo time was cut short. Groaning as the bell chimed, I placed my tray on the table, pulling my phone from my basketball shorts. Tapping the security app, my little brother was hopping from one leg to the next as Ebony stood beside him.

"Man, what da fuck?" I sighed while pressing the mic button on my screen. "Whatchall want?"

"Nigga open da doe—"

"What's da password?"

"*Tsk! Say,* bro quit playin'—It's hot as shit outchea!" Collin grumbled as I laughed, hitting the unlock button.

"Bring yo hoe ass in here... Cryin' and shit," I told them as Ebony giggled.

Hearing my alarm sing as the door opened, I lifted my tray from the coffee table and continued grinding my weed. Hearing Collin complaining about me to Ebony, they filed through the living room seconds later.

"Hey, Carter," Ebony, sweet as always, came to me with a hug.

"Man, fuck dat hoe ass nigga," Collin told her as she giggled.

"Wussup, Eb," I grinned as she plopped down on the couch near Collin as he sat on the arm.

"Nothing much..." she exhaled as her phone came out of her purse.

"Aw, shit—Bro gotchu you a new Birkin?" I noticed the orange bag as she giggled, nodding her head.

"Yeah, you know..." Ebony popped her lips as she spoke. "I gotta have my girls," she held it up in the air, twirling it around as Collin smirked.

"I gotta do somethin' to keep Shawty from askin' for a baby," Collin explained as Ebony's face cracked.

"Now, you know you lyin'!" Ebony tapped his thigh as my

brother chuckled. "That's yo ass—I'm content with this baby, right here," she beamed as she hugged the designer bag to her chest. "And the fourteen others I got... In my closet!" she grinned greedily as Collin shook his head.

"Whicho spoiled ass," Collin pinched Ebony's cheek as she giggled, swatting his hand from her face.

"You like buying me stuff," she told him before looking over at me. "Mani sleep?"

"Nah, she wit my mama and Dot," I exhaled as I rolled my blunt.

"So, they did go without me," Ebony turned towards my brother as he shrugged.

"I mean, I told you to go—"

"No, you didn't!" She giggled as Collin cracked up laughing. "You made this big ass deal about us going to eat, right then and—"

"You was hungry doe—"

"And I could've ate with Mani and mama," she rolled her eyes as Collin shook his head. "Yes, I could've."

"Look, you had yo fun for da week, fuckin' around wit Yelly," Collin spat as Ebony turned away from him. "All week y'all just up and out da house like da fuckin' Housewives on Lake Ridge," Collin's eyes shifted as he shook his head.

"I was at her shop—Not just out, drinking and fighting," Ebony rolled her eyes as Collin playfully gripped the back of her throat, pulling her to him.

"Roll dem bitches again."

Lighting my first blunt as they horsed around on my couch, I tuned everything out. If I couldn't be alone, I'd pretend like I was. Inhaling, my mind went over the to-do list for the soiree. There was a lot to do and so little time. I had the tents, the DJ, the lights, the food—Clothes and most of the decor. Set-up would be a breeze. I just needed a few more things and a couple more people to make the function complete.

"*Eh*," I felt Collin tap me as I came to. "Whatchu stressin' bout?"

"Nothin' really, just mullin' ova a few thangs," I told him as he held his hand out to get a rotation stated. "Man, c'mon—"

"Why yo ass so stingy witcho shit?" Collin laughed as I smirked, still shaking my head. "I share every time you—"

"How many times I been around you without my own shit?"

"Not many—"

"Exactly."

"Butchu act like there ain't been times, I spotted yo funky ass!" Collin had me choking as I laughed at his insults.

"Man, here," I handed my blunt over as Ebony giggled between us. "You always cryin' bout some shit."

"Just roll anotha one," Collin flicked his shoulders as he pulled from the half left.

I was gonna do dat shit anyway, I thought as I got to the green on my tray. Since I had my little brother's greedy ass here, I'd need five to pass the time.

"So, whatchu decide to go with?" Carter asked as we got a full steam going.

"Aw, shit—Hold up," I eagerly sat my rolling tray on the table, tapping my side for my phone. "Where da fuck my phone?" I asked out loud, knowing I'd just had it to let them in my house.

Seeing Amani's laptop on the other end of the table, near Collin, I tapped Ebony and watched her get up to retrieve it. Opening it, I noticed Ebony looking, so I turned to the side, shielding the screen as she giggled.

"I'on know what her screensaver is and I'on need you seein' some shit—"

"*Ew*," Ebony gagged as I laughed. "It shouldn't be nothin' on there, in the first place!"

"How you gon' dictate what we do?"

"Because y'all got kids!" Ebony countered as I nodded my head, agreeing with her.

"Cairo know better than to pick dis up, doe," I still had to add my two cents in as I pecked the password to unlock her laptop.

Waiting a second for the screen to load, I placed a blunt in my mouth and lit it. Inhaling just as the light flickered, I glanced down, frowning. Blinking as I stared back at Amani's screen, I felt my jaw tightening as I scrolled through her recent google search. *Shawty got me fucked up!* Seeing she had six more tabs open, I clicked the second nosily, ready to throw her laptop across the room as I read off an article titled: *Late-term Abortions in Illinois.*

BEEP. BEEP.

The front door opened as the foyer filled with my mama and Amani's voices. Pulling the blunt from my lips, I watched Collin do the same, only quicker. Swatting at the air, he was acting like the sneaky teenager he used to be as I dabbed my blunt.

"Oh, I know I don't smell what I think I do," my mama came into the living room with bags in her hands. "Ebony!" She stamped her foot. "I thought you were out eating—"

"We were," Ebony looked to Collin as he glared off in another direction. "But you know your son—"

"Nah, don't put dis on me," Collin cut her off as he got up to hug my mama. "Hey, lady," he kissed the side of her face as she giggled, nudging him. "What I do?"

"You know I wanted to make this a family affair—"

"I ain't know," he laughed as Ebony and my mama hit him.

"Hey, baby," Amani popped up behind me, hugging me from the back of the couch while kissing the side of my face.

I blew my whole high as I swallowed slowly, reaching for her arms to unhook them from my neck. Trying my hardest not to make it obvious, I could see my mama looking away from Collin and Ebony to watch me interact with Amani.

"Where's Dot?"

"*Oh—Uh,* I took her upstairs," Amani's eyes searched my face as hers curled in confusion. "She's sleep."

Brushing past her, I had to get out of the living room. Going straight for the nursery to process what I'd just seen. Sensing Amani on my heels, she was going to make it hard for me to keep my attitude in check.

"She's sleep—"

"I can still check," I snapped at her just as we got through the nursery doors.

"Okay—*Wait...*" Amani waved her right hand around as she shook her head slowly. "Why are you mad?"

"I ain't mad," I lied, knowing she could hear it in my tone.

"Carter, you are—"

"Stop touchin' me," I told her as she hooked her arms to mine.

"What?"

Jerking away from her as she flinched, I could see Amani on the verge of tears.

"You heard—"

"*Eh,* Nigga—C'mere!" Collin called to me as I cut my eyes at Amani, whose face was already cracked from the shock of my words.

"Whatchu want?"

"Just c'mere—I need you to ride somewhere with me," Collin was now at the base of the stairs as I walked out of the nursery. "Mama and Eb gon' stay with Mani until we get back."

"A'ight—Lemme get my shit," I told him as I turned towards my bedroom.

I'll deal with dis shit later...

CHAPTER ELEVEN

Amani

ANXIOUSLY WAITING FOR MY NAME TO BE CALLED, I tapped my toe against the carpet, looking from Carter to my hands whenever I caught his eye and he turned away from me. Something was off and he wasn't telling me, and that only worried me even more. So much so I'd been counting down the minutes until I saw Dr. Clark. My current addiction, I needed her more than my old habit of smoking. I craved our two-hour sessions like a supermodel did greasy food on her diet. She was balancing out my home life in a way I'd yearned for since my mother was alive. *Heck, I was no longer referring to my mother by her first name.* If that's no small feat, I don't know what is. Not only was seeing Dr. Clark a cure to my postpartum depression, but she was unknowingly a well on infinite answers, I asked often regarding my life. The latest being: *What happened between the time I was away with Carter's mom and when we came back?*

Because I didn't know, and he wasn't budging. *Ironic, isn't it?* Since he hated when I was passive aggressive... But here he was, doing the same exact thing, he didn't want me doing. And I told him I wouldn't overthink these kinds of things, but he was leaving me no choice. *What did I do?*

"*Carter*," I spoke his name softly as to avoid any confrontation in a public setting.

Not that he was keen on public disputes, but he wasn't even kissing me every chance he got. *Maybe I might need to get him to react so I know if he's still down for me.*

"What?" he peered over, giving me half his attention as he swiped through his phone.

"Are you okay?"

Raising his shoulders then nodding, I knew the first gesture was his true answer. Rolling my eyes as I took a deep breath, I hated when he shut me out.

"Can you just tell me whatever it is that's bothering you, Carter, because I don't wanna go through an episode—"

"What episode?" His eyes were ice cold as he glared over at me.

"This," I pointed in mid-air to emphasize what I meant. "I know you're mad at me—"

"Right," he nodded his head, and I groaned, crossing my arms over my chest.

"Okay, so tell me what I did or what you believe I'm keeping from you so we can discuss it and be over it," I suggested as his face became even colder.

"Mr. and Mrs. Banks," Kimmy interrupted our conversation as I sighed and stood to my feet.

It can wait until we're finished, anyway, I thought as I walked in front of Carter down the hallway. Opening the door,

Dr. Clark was sitting in her favorite brown chair, smiling up at me. Taking my seat, Carter shuffled through the door, two minutes later. Clasping my hands together as he took his seat beside me and leaned over to the right to rest his elbow on the arm of the loveseat, Kimmy closed the door. *It's showtime!*

Watching Dr. Clark as she pushed her frames up against her face, she was doing her normal once over of me and Carter. After which she'd jot down a few notes then start talking. But when her smile thinned as she moved her hands together, leaning in... I knew something was up.

"Is everything alright?" She asked both of us but her eyes were on Carter.

Gazing over my shoulder, he was doing everything possible to put space between us. Lowering my shoulders as I looked away from him, I didn't know what to tell her. Carter was acting weird and he wasn't going to tell me why, which defeated our purse of even being here.

"Amani?" She finally addressed me as I shook my head.

"Everything good," Carter spoke up as I kept my face forward.

"It's not and he won't tell me what's bothering him so we can fix it," I blurted out as Carter huffed next to me.

I felt and sounded like a tattling child but if this was the game my husband wanted to play... Then I'd gladly oblige. We've come too far to regress into former childish ways. And it was his idea to come here in the first place.

"Carter can you—"

"You wanna know what's botherin' me?" Carter cut Dr. Clark off as he turned towards me.

"Yes, I do," I matched his gaze, feeling like he was trying to intimidate me into fearing whatever he was withholding from me, so I'd drop it.

"A'ight," Carter nodded before looking at Dr. Clark. "So, I

go outta my way for Shawty—Every day... No matter what it is," he spoke to Dr. Clark as I listened. "And I'm not lookin' for a pat on da back cuz I signed up for dis shit—As her husband and primary provider... It's cool with me," he spoke as Dr. Clark scribbled a few things down. "Then boom—I get side-swiped with da bullshit. Mani homesick, I bring a lil piece of home here. Mani can't handle being a mother—"

"Carter don't do this," Dr. Clark has suddenly transformed from our shrink to a concern confidant.

"So, I call my cousin up," Carter ignores Dr. Clark's pleas as my eyes well up. "Get da number for her and drag her ass up here for sessions she ain't want... Everything is seemingly smooth but dats how Mani operates—"

"Are you serious right now?" The words coming from his mouth floored me.

"Do I look like I'm jokin'," he snapped as I pursed my lips together, swiping at the first tear falling from my eye. "If you ain't want dis life Shawty you could've left me alone—"

"What are you talking about?" My hands trembled as I gripped my knees to stop them from shaking. "Why would I be here if I didn't want to be?"

Stopping in the middle of his rant, Carter balled up his fists and looked away from me. *If I didn't want to be here?* Why would that be a thought in his head? Nobody leaves the city they were born and raised in to come to a new state for nothing. I don't anybody in Texas, outside of Carter's family. Yeah, I met Sha through school but had I not moved here... I wouldn't know her either. I love Carter and knew I wouldn't find anything close to what I feel when I'm with him if I allowed him to drift away.

"Carter?" I called his name, but he'd mentally checked out from this conversation.

"Dot is stayin' here," he finally spoke up without even

looking at me. "You can do whateva you want wit da otha baby," he shrugged, and I almost choked.

"Other baby?" Now I was confused. "What are you talking about—"

"Da baby you was tryna skip up to Chicago to abort," Carter cut me off as I sat back thinking. "Dats what dis shit was all about, wasn't it?"

So many thoughts were swirling through my head as I tried to make sense of what he was telling me. Nothing stopped the confusion. I felt like I was having an out-of-body experience because this wasn't me and my husband arguing over a baby. A damn baby that didn't exist. No, this had to be some skit Dr. Clark hypnotized us into reenacting.

"I'm not pregnant!" I shouted at him as he waved me off. "And that can easily be proved by peeing on a stick—Carter, I don't even have words!" I waved my hands around frantically. "A *baby*—Why would I have an abortion?"

"You ain't want Dot!" He matched my tone as I sat up straight. "It's apparent—"

"Don't!" I cut him knowing he was about to say something he'd regret. "I want her—Otherwise I wouldn't be here fighting to get better!" I pointed my finger at him. "And you brought me here, *Carter*—Why are you doing this?" I finally broke down as Dr. Clark handed me her bamboo tissue box. "Was it all for nothing—"

"Don't turn dis shit on me," Carter blew my tears off. "Ask dat nigga BJ what it was since you googling him and shit," he spat and that's when it hit me.

My *damn* laptop! *CRAP!* Pulling my phone from my purse, I felt like time was slipping. I only had one shot to prove my innocence and if I didn't hurry, Carter would walk out on me. Tapping into my email, I clicked over to blackboard to upload the paper I turned in two weeks ago for my social issues class.

Taking a deep breath, I felt like I was about to give a presentation in front of a classroom.

"Yes, I searched Brandon—And I was wrong, but it wasn't for the reasons you believe," I started off, wishing Carter would just look at me. "He emailed me a couple weeks back..." I exhaled, and that was the thing that got Carter's attention.

Snapping his neck in my direction, I could see the hurt he masked with anger in his fiery eyes. That hurt because I was wrong for even searching Brandon in the first place.

"I didn't respond to him—"

"So, why did you look him up?" Dr. Clark interjected as I glanced over at her before shrugging.

"I don't know," I sighed heavily. "*I—He...* We were friends long before I met Carter and I guess I just wanted to see how he was doing."

I could hear Carter scoffing as I bared my whole heart to Dr. Clark. This wasn't an easy thing for me to admit, but I wanted to do it for us. Hindsight is 20/20 because looking back on it... Nothing I said today would justify my decision to google Brandon. Which meant I still had a little love left to let go of for him.

"Did you two ever—"

"Yes," I didn't even have to hear the entire question to know how to answer.

"And you loved—"

"*Tsk!*" Carter smacked his lips as he shot up from the loveseat, startling me. "I'm not finna sit here and listen to dis shit!" He stormed out without giving me or Dr. Clark a chance to stop him.

Bursting into tears, I knew this was the last straw for him. I lost him and it was my fault. Dropping my face into my hands as I cried like a baby, I could feel my heart straining as I internally beat myself up.

"I never planned on replying," I sobbed to Dr. Clark as I lifted my snotty face. "I know I should've deleted his message but—"

"But why didn't you?" She pushed me to the edge.

"Because I finally got what I wanted," I blurted out. "After twelve years of friendship, watching him go through women like water—Developing a crush and sleeping with him... Only to be tossed aside like every other girl in his life," I sniffled. "He broke and reached out to me. Apologized and fawned after me —Like I wanted when I wanted him," I admitted to Dr. Clark as I heard my own words. "*When I wanted him...*" I repeated as an epiphany hit.

"Right," Dr. Clark smirked as I slowly dropped my head to my hands.

"*Yeah...*" I breathed, knowing this was what I needed to realize all along. "But after the shock of his random email wore off—"

"You didn't feel like you thought you would?" she finished my sentence with a question as I nodded my head up and down.

"Yeah," I looked to the tethered tissue in my hand. "I didn't want his attention nor his apology," I laughed in the middle of crying. "Can you believe that?" I couldn't stop laughing. "I used to cry to my sisters about this guy—Depressed and hardly eating, and now I'm disgusted with myself for even getting into bed with him," I dry gagged as Dr. Clark smirked. "And you know what's even funnier?"

"What's that?"

"Instead of writing him back, I thought, *lemme look him up and see how he's doing,*" I mimicked my thoughts. "Then I came across this picture of him and some woman—He was kissing and hugging on her so I'm sure she's his girlfriend," I took a deep breath before revealing the true kicker. "But he still sent me that disingenuous email. Which means, not only hasn't he changed—"

"But he's playing his new woman, too."

"Exactly," I pointed my finger while nodded. "And that's when it really hit me that I'd dodged a bullet and even better... *Well*, what was..." I stopped talking as another twinge of sadness crept up on me.

"He's not going to leave you," Dr. Clark told me as she handed me another Kleenex.

"I know you're supposed to say things to make me feel better, but I'd prefer you don't," I told Dr. Clark as she laughed.

"Is that what you think I studied for six years to get these three degrees for?" She asked me as my shoulders rose. "I'm not a paid friend, Amani—I'm a therapist. I'm here to help you through your problems, not coddle you," Dr. Clark's smile was gone and her tone was heavier. "I listen and assess and suggest and prescribe—None of my methods are intended to make you comfortable... They get you talking, analyzing and moving on with your life. Hence the reason you're still here, open and receptive and learning—You probably would've gon' on inside your head behind Carter not speaking to you without opening your mouth to call him on it," she knew the old me so well as I quietly listened to her. "But you picked up some new gems, here—And you sharpened your communication skills," she told me as a new, brighter smile appeared on her face. "And not only that, you're more observant of your husband—And not how you thought you were before," she was right. "You picked up on his mood right from the second it changed, didn't you?" Dr. Clark asked me as my mind flashed back to to me coming home with Carter's mama as I nodded my head. "That's my job. That's what I'm supposed to do—That's how I know he's not leaving you—Nor are you going anywhere but let this serve as a lesson to you, Amani, girl. Let go of your sordid past if you want to maintain anything good in the future."

Staring into her eyes, I didn't have any words, and it was for the best. I didn't need to say anything. Dr. Clark was laying it on thick, and I needed this coat for the chill Carter had given me.

"You're your own worse enemy because you sabotage everything good in your life over something you had no control of when you were younger," she told me as my bottom lip quivered. "Let your mother's death be the end of this—Because you deserve the happiness you've gained," she gave me another tissue. "You don't have to keep begging for scraps in people like Brandon... Because you've paid for your past in guilt now let it be," her voice cracked like thunder and struck me. "Has Fatima forgiven you?"

"Yes."

"So, repeat after me...I—"

"*I.*"

"Forgive."

"*Forgive.*"

"Me."

"*Me.*"

Like water bursting through a damn, tears fell from my eyes. Drawing in huge breaths as my chest expanded. At first, I thought I was struggling to breathe, but then I started laughing. *Laughing!* Face stretching to make room for all thirty-two teeth showing. I could feel my heart fluttering as a wave of newfound peace settled into my spirit. Oh, *my goodness!* I fanned my hands out because I couldn't contain myself.

"Let it out!" Dr. Clark joined me by fanning me as she laughed, too. "This is also my job, honey—It's called a breakthrough!"

Jumping up from my seat, my arms enclosed around Dr.

Clark as she gasped then hugged me back. Still crying, I wasn't sad anymore. These were actually tears of joy. *This is how I felt like giving birth!* I thought as I squeezed Dr. Clark tighter.

"Thank you for—*God,* I needed this!" I finally pulled back from her as I took my seat, again.

"This is what I'm here for," Dr. Clark chuckled as I swiped my face clean with a fresh Kleenex. "Now, go find your husband and talk it out—Because I want an apology from him for storming out!" she told me as I giggled and nodded.

"Okay!" I stood up with Dr. Clark, hugging her again before I left as she snickered.

Emerging from the clinic doors with a new attitude, I scanned the parking lot for Carter's truck. Blocking the sun with my hands, I heard an engine creeping up behind me and turned to see Carter pulling to the curb. Sucking in air through my nostrils, I was confident in myself that Carter and I would be okay. *Because I wasn't letting him walk out on me that easily.*

CHAPTER TWELVE

Carter

Pushing through the plexiglass door, I could feel my face burning from the rage and sun. I'd been holding in this shit about Amani's secret abortion search and BJ's google pics all night. With Amani suffocating me with her questions and gazes because she knew I was pissed off at her. Now that I got it out in the open, I didn't feel as constricted. I could breathe and think a little better too. Shawty sat in there and acted out a whole lie. Coming down here for what? Just to cry on her phone to her sisters about a nigga who never paid her dust.

RING!

Feeling for my phone, I found it in my right side pocket. Glancing down at the number, it had a Chicago area code. Inhaling deeply, I put it to my ear. I didn't want to sound angry on the phone, even though this sudden call from Chicago only made me angrier with Amani.

"Hello?"

"Yeah, I gotta call from dis number?" A woman answered as I thought for a second.

"Yeah—I think I called da wrong..." I stopped mid-sentence to try another approach. "You know a muhfucka named *Julian*?"

"Yeah, I do," she giggled at the way I addressed him. "But he ain't here and dis ain't his phone—Dats my daddy."

"Aw, my fault, Shawty," I found myself smirking too, knowing exactly who I was speaking with. "Can you give him my number and tellem it's urgent."

"Yeah, I can do dat," she agreed as I picked up on the seduction in her voice.

From my brief time at Julian's house, before Amani ran out on her family, I could sense some tension between this girl and my wife. She was eager to talk over her and I caught Shawty rolling her eyes every time Amani spoke or somebody, in their family, asked her a question. She was only nice to me and I knew what that shit was all about.

"Wuss yo name?"

"*Solomon*," I gave her my middle, knowing she would know who I was if I didn't.

"Solomon... *Okay*, he'll hitchu up later," she promised as I ended the call.

Stuffing my phone back into my pocket, I felt like a hot ass fool standing in front of this building. After this phone call, I wasn't even angry anymore. Just disappointed with Amani. Taking a long breath, I started walking to my truck. These over a hundred degree days were no joke. And no temper was worth a heat stroke. Pushing the engine button and raising the blast from the air conditioner, I reclined my seat back to cool off. Breathing slowly, I closed my eyes and thought long and hard about my next move.

I had life decisions to make behind this stunt Amani pulled. Was what we had worth the drama? Stressing out every other week because she had some new shit going on she didn't know how to deal with. I mean, the postpartum was understandable, but these lingering feelings she had for BJ could fuck us up in the long run. I wasn't normally a jealous nigga, but I'd invested everything into me and Amani because I loved her. Shawty had my nose wide open, and she was still shitting on me.

"Dis ain't it," I told myself as I pulled my seat up to look out the window.

Watching the door, I could see Amani emerge from it after fifteen minutes of alone time with Dr. Clark. Judging by the smile plastered on her face, I knew this was just what she needed. Despite the bullshit I found on her laptop, Amani was finally blossoming in my city and it was a beautiful thing to witness.

Switching gears as Amani searched the lot, I crept up on her slowly from behind. Knowing she'd hear me, I waited for her to turn around instead of blaring the horn. Watching her take a deep breath, I did the same and got out the truck. Walking Amani to the passenger's side, I opened her door and helped her in as she thanked me, knowing I was still giving her the silent treatment.

Getting back in, Amani was twisting the knob to the air conditioner as she looked my way. Inhaling, I already knew what was coming before she started up.

"Carter..." she touched the hand I always rested between

us. “Look at me,” she reached for my chin, but I jerked away from her. “I’m not pregnant—See,” she flashed her phone in my face as I swatted her hand away. “Why are you trying to have an attitude with me—”

“I’m not tryin’ shit, Shawty,” I cut her off as I left the curb. “You shoulda thought about dis shit when you searched dat nigga up after he reached out to you—”

“Okay and I’m sorry, Carter—That was wrong and I shouldn’t have,” she admitted her fault as my jaw clenched. “I didn’t think I still had feelings for him, but I did...” she dropped her head in shame as I balled my right hand into a first. “But they weren’t the feelings I thought,” she looked to me as I turned to see her face. “I wanted him to gravel and beg for my forgiveness—To realize I was a prize while I went on with my life with you... And like a fool, I didn’t consider your feelings while I used our love to seek revenge.”

Driving and listening to her explain her actions, the love I still had for her overpowered my anger. Yeah, it was tough hearing she used me to get back at that nigga but I could hear her sincerity. She wanted to make amends.

“I’m just now learning how to be content with what I have —All the good I have,” she corrected herself as I turned into Chick-Fil-A. “And I’m not going to make excuses for what I’ve done—None of it,” she vowed as I kept my face forward, creeping through the drive-thru. “But I want you to know every time I tell you I love you, I mean it.”

“It’s a great day at Chick-Fil-A—This is Kelsey, how may I serve you?”

“How you doin’ Kelsey,” I ignored Amani’s declaration of love and it kind of crushed my spirit a little, but I didn’t let it show.

“I’m fine—How about yourself?”

“I’m better now,” I chuckled with the cashier.

"Well, that's nice to hear—What can I get for you, sir?"

"Lemme get a twelve count with fries and a sweet tea."

My face hung outside my window as I scanned over the menu. Knowing what Amani usually got, I didn't have to turn to look at her. Plus, I didn't want to see the look on her face after I ignored her. She was probably crying or close to it.

"Okay and the sauce?"

"Barbecue and buffalo," I responded as my phone buzzed. "And then..." I paused to look at the screen.

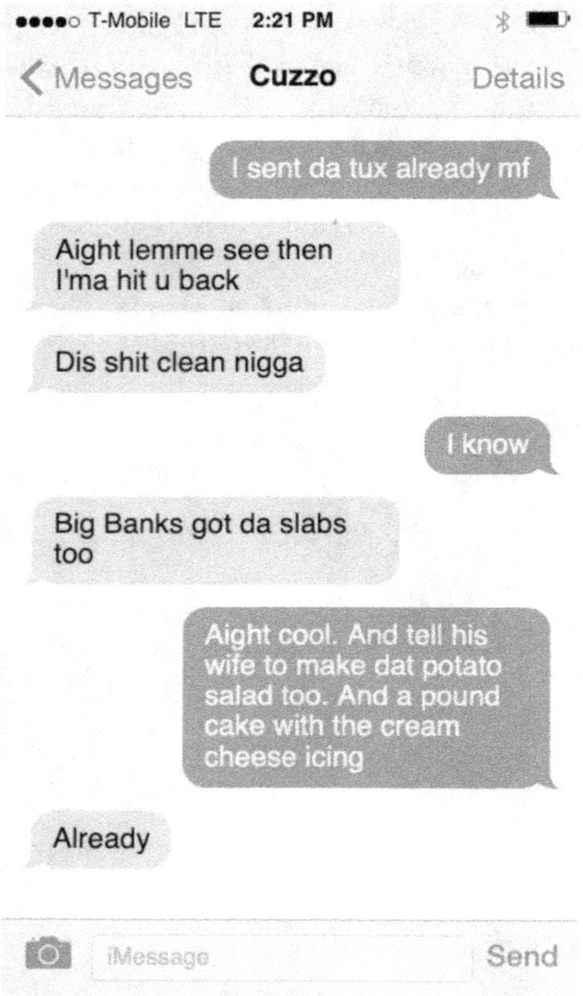

●●●●○ T-Mobile LTE 2:21 PM
Messages
Cuzzo
Details
I sent da tux already mf
Aight lemme see then I'ma hit u back
Dis shit clean nigga
I know
Big Banks got da slabs too
Aight cool. And tell his wife to make dat potato salad too. And a pound cake with the cream cheese icing
Already
iMessage
Send

Sliding my phone into the cup holder, I turned my attention back to the menu.

"Lemme get a spicy southwest salad with da fried nuggets and avocado dressing and an Arnold Palmer," I told Kelsey.

"*Okay*—Anything else?"

"Nope, dassit."

"*Eighteen-Oh-Seven,* is your total—I'll see you at the window!"

Inching my truck forward, like always, Chick-Fil-A was packed. Even with the drive-thru moving along, I don't think I've ever been here with less than twenty cars. Taking five minutes to get to the window, I paid for our food and drove off. Quietly riding through traffic, Amani didn't speak another word to me the entire way home. I guess she got the memo. I just needed her to chill while I got over this shit. I still loved her but she was in the doghouse until further notice.

"Thank you," she said as I helped her out the truck.

Nodding my head, Amani followed behind me up the steps and through the front door. She stayed by me until we came into the kitchen. Plopping down on one of the island stools, I opened my nuggets and got to work. Still ignoring her as she picked at her salad, staring daggers at my forehead.

"Are you seriously going to ignore me all day?" She asked as I swallowed my food, then took a sip from my drink. "Carter!" Amani groaned, trying to get me to talk back to her. "Do you want a divorce?"

She was trying to bait me and I almost said something, but I stopped myself. Still, I know she could see the look on my face and knew I had feelings for her. Just not in the mood to be bothered.

"You know... This is just great," she blew out a breath. "If I did this to you—There'd be hell fire with the way you'd huff and puff until I gave in," she slapped her palms against the granite. "But now that the shoe is on the other foot... You're pulling away, shutting me out, and acting like a baby—"

"I ain't hit no other bitch up, doe—"

"You didn't have to," she cut me off as I glared in her direction.

"What—"

"*Gotcha!*" Amani flashed all her teeth while pointing at me as I kept my expression bleak.

Shaking my head, "Dis ain't no fuckin' joke, Mani—"

"I know that, but you won't talk to me, so I can make it right!" she whined as I pushed my nugget carton away.

"I'on wanna forgive you right now!" I snapped as she flinched from the sound of my voice. "You can look sad all you want, Mani but leave me alone."

Watching her bottom lip quiver, I turned away so I wouldn't see her crying. I'd had enough of that shit anyway—

SMACK!

Amani's salad tray hit just below my chin, splattering salad dressing all over my shirt as it fell to the countertop and floor. Infuriated, I damn near jumped over the island to get to her. Snatching Amani up as she tried to make a run for it.

"What da fuck is wrong witchu?" I growled into her face.

"Since you wanna stay mad... Now you have more incentive to do so," she frowned as my grip on her arms grew tighter.

"*Say*, Shawty—I'ma fuck you up!" I snarled as her shoulders rose and fell. "You'on care—"

"Nope!"

"Clean dis shit up—"

"*Fuck* you," Amani rolled her eyes as my blood continued to boil.

"Fuck me?" I used her words as she nodded her head up and down.

Close to breathing fire as my chest heaved, Amani's gaze was just as hot as mine. The room was sweltering from the heat of the moment... It felt like the second time we fucked. Backing Amani up against the wall, she was just as much into as I was. Running her fingers through my hair as she pulled my face into hers, I released one of her arms to wrap her hair around my hand. Forcefully tugging at her hair, she grunted as her head tilted to the side, exposing her neck. Plunging into her skin, I could hear her moans as I trailed kisses down to her collarbone before lifting her body up.

The rougher I was with her the better I felt. Not to mention the more Amani responded with the same fire. Biting, squeezing, scratching and ripping each other's clothes off. Since she wanted to play... We gon' play all night. *Then she gon' clean dis shit up off my floor!*

CHAPTER THIRTEEN

Amani

Feeling the sun baking my face, I lied awake with my eyes closed. My entire body was warm from the rays and heat from Carter holding onto me. Naked as the day we came into this world, I loved waking up like this. Skin-to-skin, there was something so intimate about touching this way... Something not too many people reveled in. *I guess that's why they recommend it to new mothers.*

Still, how we ended up like this was far from innocent. Smirking as a flashback of the night we shared replayed in my head, I could feel a tingling in the pit of my stomach. Rough, angry sex was one of the best ways to relieve the tension.

Opening my eyes, I caught a glimpse of the clock and frowned. Carter had me up until four and it was already three in the afternoon. Normally, I'd rise early enough to see the sun sitting on the horizon because I was so used to being up from working downtown.

Buzzzz!

I looked to the side table where my phone was lying, unhooking Carter's arms from my stomach so I could get to it. Snatching me up just as I freed myself, I giggled as he dug his face into the crook of my neck. Raining down kisses on me was the last thing he should've been doing. I was already sore and I don't think I could go so soon after last night, either. Honestly, I was good for a couple days.

"My phone," I whined as he continued squeezing and kissing me. "Carter—"

"*Mm-mmm,*" he hummed into my ear as I shivered.

Feeling him squeezed my butt, I giggled as he moved the around to my mound. Clenching my legs together, I was shaking my head as he chuckled.

"Carter!" I shrieked as he pried my legs open, arching my back a little. "Stop!"

"*Mm-mmm,*" he kept moaning as I looked over my shoulder trying to see his face.

He was still hiding in my neck, ignoring me as I gripped his hands to pull them from my legs. Laughing as he strained, I wasn't going to win this fight.

"I can't—"

"Why not?" his brassy voice was louder in ear.

"Because," I sighed as his fingers brushed against my clit.

"Because what?"

"I'm sore."

"*Mm-mmm*," Carter went back to the way he was responding before inserting one of his fingers into me as I gasped.

Wincing at first. The longer he did it, the better it felt as I ground my butt into his pelvis. Matching his movement with each hand motion, Carter didn't spend too long using his fingers before he pulled out. Taking one of his hands behind me, I could feel him stroking and gripping himself as he used the other hand to lift my leg.

"Sss..." My shoulders tensed as he pressed the tip of his dick to my opening.

"Just relax," he instructed like I wasn't already trying to. "Stop squeezin'—"

"*Ahhh!*" I squeaked as he slid himself through.

DING. DONG.

Buzzz!

Pushing myself off him, Carter slid out unintentionally as I giggled. Snatching my phone from the side table just as he grabbed me again, I pressed the button to pick up.

"Hello?" I swatted his hands away from my body as he smacked his lips, still going for what he wanted.

"Amani—Where are you?" Mrs. Banks sounded relieved to hear my voice.

"*Ma*?" I shocked to hear her as I pulled the phone from my ear to read her name across my screen. "Hi," I giggled nervously, pushing Carter away as he seemed unfazed by his mother calling. "I'm at home."

Trying not to laugh as Carter pinned me down, I was fighting a losing battle with one hand to his chest and the other keeping my phone to my ear. In one swift motion, he was back inside of me as a long breath blew from my mouth.

"Well, let *us* in! I've been standing out here knocking for ten minutes and Dot's burning up—"

"*OH MY GOD!*" I jerked up, knowing my head into Carter's as he grunted.

"*Shit*—Mani!"

"I'm sorry!" I giggled as I rubbed my forehead, dropping my phone to rub the side of his head where mine collided. "Your mom and Dot have been outside in the sun—"

"What?" Carter pulled out.

"*Yeah*—She said she was knocking!" I briefed him as we both jumped out of bed.

Shifting the clothes around on the floor, I tossed my dress over my head and ran out the room. Carter was still jumping into his jeans as I made it to the bottom of the steps. Hearing his feet as my hand touched the doorknob and twisted.

"I'm so sorry, Ma—I didn't hear you," I apologized as soon as I got the door open.

Dot was screaming as Mrs. Banks same through the door. Feeling bad, I hated we didn't hear them. I mean, I heard my phone buzzing, but I didn't think much of it.

"I see why you didn't hear me," Mrs. Banks pointed out my disheveled hair and clothing as I grinned guiltily. "And you," she pointed towards the stairs as I looked over my shoulder to see Carter coming down.

"What?" He smirked, taking the car seat from her hand.

"You know what—"

"Ma, I told you about comin' here tryna run shit," Carter blew out a sigh as he led the way into the kitchen.

Placing Dot's seat on the countertop, I went to the fridge for a bottle, forgetting about the mess I'd created yesterday.

Gasping as I noticed a trail of ants, Carter's mama came around the island to see what I saw.

"Oh my goodness!" she turned towards her son as he pointed back at me.

"Ask her why it's like dat," Carter egged it on as I rolled my eyes before turning to open the fridge for a bottle.

"I made a little mess, I forgot to clean up—"

"Nah, you made a big mess, you told me you weren't gon' clean up," Carter corrected me as I slapped Dot's bottle on the counter. "Nah, don't get mad—Own yo shit, Mani, remember?"

"*Yes*—I remember," I cinched my lips as I spoke, causing Carter to laugh. "*Tattletale*," I mumbled underneath my breath as Carter gripped my shoulder in a Vulcan hold.

Feeling my knees weaken as I squealed laughing, Carter wouldn't let me go.

"Say dat shit again—"

"Carter!" I laughed with him.

"You play too much!" I pushed him as soon as he released me.

"Quit talkin' shit, Mani," he warned as I rolled my eyes to the side.

"Did y'all have a food fight?" Mrs. Banks giggled before she noticed the look on me and her son's faces. "Oh—"

Grabbing the broom from the pantry, I got to work cleaning up my mess. Spraying the ants with soapy water, they dispersed as I made a mental note to call an exterminator. We didn't have much of a bug problem... May a few ants and tiny scorpions here and there—But I wanted to make sure there was a barrier around the house so this wouldn't happen.

By the time I was finished, Carter had Amani cradled in his arms fighting her sleep. Talking to his mama about their family, I'd tuned them out during my cleaning.

"Squeaky clean," Carter teased as I came from the pantry after putting the broom back.

"Shut up," I giggled just as Dot lifted her head up to look at me.

"*Uh-Uhn,* lay down!" Carter tried pushing her head back as she squirmed and whimpered.

Reaching for me, I was shocked. Blinking, as Dot continued trying to get to me, Carter lifted her in the air for me to grab her. Taking Dot into my arms, she smiled. It hadn't been the first time I held her since going to therapy, but this was the first time she wanted me over Carter. Smiling back at her, she cooed the same way she did when she was in her father's arms. Melting from her sweetness, Dot gripped the straps of my dress before digging her head into my chest. Feeling my heart flutter, I'd watched her do this a million times with Carter.

"Hey!" Carter poked Dot's back as she snapped her head in his direction. "Whatchu doin' allat for?" he questioned her as she giggled like she understood he was joking. "Nah, I ain't laughin', lil Shawty—Dats our thang!"

Placing the palm of my hand to the back of her head, I gently pressed Dot into me as she buried her face into my bosoms. *My baby!* I gushed as my lips spread to reveal my teeth.

"She's so sleepy," Mrs. Banks spoke up as I nodded my head, still caught up in the moment.

"I'll rock her to sleep," I told her as I kissed the top of Dot's sweet head.

My little red-haired, freckle-face, green-eyed little girl finally wanted me. I could feel myself beaming as I made a note to tell Dr. Clark. She really helped me out of my funk. Kissing Dot's head again, I made my way out of the kitchen, hearing Carter right behind me until his mother called him. Turning to look over my shoulder, I laughed, sticking out my tongue as I kept going.

Up the stairs and into the nursery, Dot never took her eyes off me and the feeling was stupendous. In a calmer state, I could see my daughter as she was—Not screaming at the top of her lungs all red in the face trying to get away from me... And I loved it. Plopping down on the rocking chair, I sat Dot up, facing me as she grinned.

"I'm so sorry..." I told her as my shoulders loosened. "I know you'll never remember how it was before, but I want you to know mommy is better and you did that," I kissed the side of her face. "I can't believe I have you, Dot!" I gushed, stunned because she was mine. "I have a daughter," I could feel myself tearing up as Dot squealed laughing. "Yeah—I know!" I pulled her into me as warmth radiated throughout my body. "I love you so, so, so, so, so, so—"

"*Oout!*" Dot added as I giggled.

"Yes!" I beamed, still holding her close to my heart, now rocking in the chair. "So much."

After my declaration of love to my daughter, I didn't say another word. Slow and steady, we rocked. And rocked. And I patted her back softly as my thoughts drifted to hopeful thoughts of the future. Wondering how her voice would sound once she starting speaking. If she'd be a shy girl like me or a ball of magnetic energy like her father. She was already hilarious, like Carter. If anything, I hope she takes after Carter in the character department. He's fearless, and I wanted that for my baby girl, too. She had an entire world to conquer, and she'd need his confidence to do all the great things she was destined to do. *Throw in my drive and intellect and discipline.*

Gazing down at Dot, she was out cold. Mouth agape and drooling like her daddy. Kissing her sweaty forehead, she was like him in this way too. They were hot sleepers, but they wanted to hug up on you as they slept. That's why Carter kept the air on 66 with the ceiling fan on. So he could pull me into his arms and pass out.

"Whatchall in here—"

"*Shhh,*" I shushed Carter as he came into the nursery causing Dot to jerk in her sleep. "I just got her to sleep," I whispered as he helped me out of the rocking chair.

Kissing her face one more time, I slowly lowered her into the crib, moving the three bears and blanket from around her. Removing her pants, I checked her diaper, debating whether to take her shirt off too. Deciding not to, I could lower the temperature in here and turn on her fan. This way she'd stay sleep long enough to get her rest.

"C'mon," I motioned for Carter to follow me out of the nursery as he grabbed my hand, walking behind me.

Closing the door halfway, Carter twirled me around towards him. Gazing into my eyes before he leaned in to kiss me.

"I'm proud of you, Shawty," he told me as I beamed. "And I love you—"

"*Ugh!*" I pinched him as he laughed.

"I'ma always beat you to it," Carter promised as he lifted me over his shoulder. "Always!" He carried me down the hall into our bedroom as I giggled.

God, I love this man!

CHAPTER FOURTEEN

Carter

WATCHING MANI TWIRL IN FRONT OF HER MIRROR FOR the sixth time, I groaned as she giggled. Shawty knew she was getting on my nerves. *I'm bout to drag her out da house like dis,* I thought as she looked back at me smirking.

"A'int shit funny, Shawty—C'mon!"

"I'm just trying to see how I look—"

"You been seein' for ten minutes now!" My patience was gone.

"It has not been that long—"

"Amani!" I called her name as she giggled.

"Okay," she bit down on her bottom lip as she twirled for the last time. "You can't buy me a pretty dress and not expect me to marvel in it!" She gleamed as I smirked, shrugging it off.

"You ready?" My voice was softer as Amani came to my side, grabbing my hand as she lied her head against my arm.

"Yes, *daddy!*" She grinned while looking up at me.

"You better quit playin'," I flicked her chin, knowing I wasn't gonna do shit on account of me being on a schedule.

"Or else?" She countered like I knew she would.

Tensing up as I tried to show restraint, I had to keep my eyes on the prize. The prize that would take place once we came back from our fake date.

"C'mon cuz we already runnin' late," I said instead as Amani's face cracked.

"Where are we going, anyway?" She was a little let down by my rejection to her advances.

If only she knew how hard it was for me to turn her down. If she wasn't spinning in that damn mirror for half an hour, maybe I could've had her ass bent over before we left. *Shit, I could still fuck her in da car...*

"You'll see once we get there," I told her, knowing I had no true place in mind.

The plan was to drive around until I found something out of the ordinary to do. Something that would keep Amani and me busy while my mama and rest of my family set shit up for the soiree.

"I'm kinda hungry," Amani said as she let my hand go to turn in the kitchen's direction.

Quickly snatching her up, she laughed. *I'on know what made me think Amani would make dis shit easy for me.* Her suspicious ass knows something is up... That's why I need to get her out the house ASAP.

"We can grab somethin' on da way," I told her as she poked out her bottom lip. "Fix ya face for I give you somethin' to be mad about," I playfully threatened her as she grinned.

"You keep making these idle threats, Carter–*You know I'm bout dat action*!" she bumped her hip into mine as we neared the front door.

"Bout dat action," I repeated as I smacked my lips, cutting my eyes over at her. "Yeah, right–"

"I can hang!" She giggled as we got close to the car.

"Yeah... Yo ass can hang it up!" I groaned as she doubled over laughing.

"Stop it!" Amani cackled while I helped her into her seat. "You can't seem to get enough," Amani pushed her lips out as I bit them causing her eyes to bulge. "*Ugh*–"

"Shut up–You like dat shit," I flicked her chin as she coyly shrugged then giggled. "Freaky ass–"

"Still doesn't change the fact that you can't get enough–"

"Likin' da feelin' and puttin' it down on me are two different thangs," I spat as she gasped.

Closing her door, I left Amani in shock as I sauntered to the driver's side. Hearing the doors lock as my hand touched the handle, I exhaled slowly, hearing her laughing inside the car.

"Mani, quit playin'–"

"NOPE!" She yelled with all the windows rolled up.

She must've forgotten I had the key in my hand.Popping the lock and jerking the handle, I climbed in, reaching for her face to pull her into me.

"I was just–"

"Playin' too much," I squeezed her cheeks as she giggled. "Cut it out, Mani."

Staring into her eyes before she rolled them, I smirked and let her go. Doing her usual arms crossed over her chest as I started the car and pulled off, I didn't ask her about it until we were out of Lake Ridge.

"Wuss wrong witchu?"

"Are you tryna say I don't put it down?" She asked as I swerved from almost laughing in her face.

"*What*?"

"That's what you said—"

"*Tsk!* No—" I cut her off, cracking a smile as she groaned loudly. "Chill, Mani... I was just playin', Shawty." I told her as she rolled her eyes again. "*Aw*, now look who feelin's hurt after all dis shit you was doin' to me—"

"So, what?" Amani shrugged as I poked her cheek.

"You not gon' smile?"

"No."

Poking my lip out as I hung my head down, I could see the corner of Amani's lip quivering as she tried to fight the feeling. Giving her the puppy dog eyes, she burst out laughing.

"Stop—I'm mad at you!" She giggled, shoving me as I pulled into Collin and Ebony's complex. "Why are we here? I thought you said we were gonna eat!"

"Aw, shit, I forgot," I told her, still parking my car. "C'mon, we can eat inside," I told her as I got out.

Helping Amani out, I held her hand as we walked up to my brother's condo. Using my key, I watched Amani's eyes squint suspiciously. *I shoulda just took her ass to Waffle House or some place else.*

"Are they here?" She asked me, but I knew she already knew the answer before I shook my head. "Then I don't wanna be here—"

"We can go..." I told her while gripping her waist. "After you show me all dat action you about."

"This is why you stopped?" Amani shrieked as I nodded

my head. "For a quickie in your brother's house—*Carter*!" She was acting like we hadn't done it in stranger places.

I mean, not out in the open—*Well*, we christened the pool a month ago, but three months prior to that, Amani was in the guest closet with me at my parents's house begging for more. So I don't know where this new attitude is coming from.

"You was talkin' big shit back home, Mani—C'mon..." I lifted her hands to my neck as she giggled bashfully. "You want me to play some music?" I asked her as she shook her head. "A'ight then c'mon—"

"No!"

"*Fine*... I see how it is," I hung my head in jest as she snickered. "Nah, I'm playin', Shawty—"

"No, you're not!" she cut in.

"Nah, for real." My tongue wet my lips as I gazed into her brown eyes. "We ain't gotta fuck—Just brush up on a nigga, doe," I shook her softly as she giggled. "Hug me and sway!"

"Hug you and sway?"

"Dats what I said!"

"Okay," Amani slid her arms around my neck, but she was still leaning back. "Now what—"

"C'mere," I jerked her into me, tired of playing with her ass.

Pressing her head into my chest, Amani exhaled, and I started rocking us side to side. Slow and steady. No music in the background... Just her ear to my heart. That was the best sound she could hear.

"Whatchu doin'?" I asked her as she pulled back.

Without answering, Amani lifted her body with her toes and pressed her lips to the tip of my nose. Like a light switch flickering on and drowning out the darkness, my smile brightened the entire room. Reflecting my expression, Amani's face illuminated as she smiled back at me.

Dipping my face into the crook of her neck, I inhaled, remembering why I loved this part of her body the most. It held her scent and her skin was always soft.

"Whatchu got on?" I mumbled, seeing my lips were now glued to the skin of her neck.

Feeling the vibrations from her giggles as her right shoulder shuddered as a reaction to the sucking I was doing. Amani hummed then went silent, so I had no choice but pull back from my favorite spot to look at her.

"You like it?" She purred as I dove back into her neck, causing her to squeal with laughter.

Inhaling more of this unfamiliar scent. Whatever it was, Mani could get it every day she wore it. Soon as it hit my nostrils, I was gone tear her ass up.

"C'mon, let's watch a movie or somethin'," I suggested before my thoughts became too x-rated.

"We could've done that at home," she told me as I shook my head. "And why not?"

"Cuz bro Netflix is better—"

"Shut up!" Amani laughed with me.

Bringing her over to the couch with me, Amani never took her eyes off my face. She was trying to figure out what I had planned, but she'd never find out until it was time.

"You can stop lookin' at me—"

"Why?"

"Cuz we finna watch, *Umbrella Academy*—"

"Ew!" she gagged as I playfully clutched my chest.

"Whatchu mean, *ew*?"

"I don't like it—"

"Nah... You don't just say dat..." I shook my head as Amani giggled. "My wife not finna sit here and disrespect da kids—"

"Carter!" Amani cackled. "I don't want to watch Netflix!" she groaned.

“Whatchu wanna do—”

“You know what I wanna do—And if you make any reference to sex, I’m taking an Uber back home!” she threatened as I pressed my palm to my chest.

“You gon’ what?”

“I’m not—”

“A’ight, Shawty,” I chuckled as Amani rolled her eyes. “Let’s go feed my baby,” I told her while rubbing her stomach.

“Ain’t no baby in here,” Amani retorted as we stood up.

“I know—You my baby,” I winked causing her to blush. “You still my baby?”

“Kinda—”

“Ain’t no kinda,” I snapped as she giggled. “Yo ass,” I shook my head as I let her lead to the door.

Opening and letting us out, I set Collin’s alarm and locked up behind us. Taking Amani’s hand back into mine, I figured if I got something in her stomach and talked, we’d waste an hour or two. That should be enough time.

“C’mere,” I pulled Amani’s hand just as we reached my car. “I love you,” I told her while pecking her lips. “You look beautiful, too.”

“What are you up to?” She finally asked as I shook my head, keeping my expression bleak.

“Nothin’, Shawty—I just wantchu to feel special today and every day... But since you been progressin’ in therapy,” I exhaled as she smiled. “Dis lil time out is a reward—”

“A reward?”

“Yeah, you know—Somethin’ to keep you on da right track,” I told her as she nodded slowly. “Plus, with Dot monopolizing all yo time—”

“She is not!” Amani giggled as I pressed my lips to hers, again.

"She is—You'on be seein' da looks lil Shawty give me when you refuse to put her down but she know what she doin'!"

"Shut up, Carter," Amani nudged me as I smirked.

"Nah, but I'm proud of you."

Watching her eyes flutter as she looked to the side, I gripped her chin, redirecting her eye-line with mine. It's been a crazy ass ride since the first night I met Shawty and I wouldn't dream of getting off now. And the fact that we got through her postpartum, together—With no outside help from our family and friends just proved our marriage would stand the test of time.

"I can't take all the credit, though," Amani told me as I shrugged and inhaled, like I didn't know where she was getting at. "Stop!" Amani giggled. "I'm serious—"

"I know, Shawty but dats my job—Through sickness and in health," I vowed and would stand firm on that shit.

Watching Amani's smile widen, I mirrored it. Taking in a deep breath, she let in out revealing even more teeth.

"How did I get so lucky—"

"I'on know," I shrugged nonchalantly. "I ask God every day how Mani get a nigga like me—"

"You know..." Amani held up her finger condescendingly. "I asked Him that very same thing, too!" She laughed with me as I walked us over to her side of the car.

"And what he say?" I played along.

"He ain't get back to me yet..." she sighed as I opened her door. "I guess I'll ask again, after ten years."

"Just ten?"

"Yeah, well—I was thinking... Maybe I'd make it a decade thing," she explained as I nodded my head. "Every time we hit another ten, I'll see if he gives me the answer."

"*A'ight*—Deal," I shook on it and doubled over laughing

with my wife. "I love you," I pecked her lips as she coyly melted into her seat.

"I love you, too—But can I say it first, one day?"

"Nope—But you'll be a'ight," I told her as she dropped her shoulders. "Buckle up!" I yelled out as I closed the door.

CHAPTER FIFTEEN

Amani

COMING THROUGH THE FRONT DOOR LAUGHING AT Carter, my stomach and heart were full. It was only a quarter to two, and I was ready to crash from the itis. Waffle House had to be my favorite place to eat since I came to Dallas. Grits, ham, scrambled eggs with cheese, and a two stack. Oh, and don't forget my hash browns and ketchup.

"I'm so sleepy," I told Carter as we walked to the stairs. "You gonna go to bed with me?"

"Yeah—Lemme go put dis in da fridge," he told me, kissing my lips before turning me loose.

Taking one step at a time, I was trying to give Carter a

chance to meet me halfway. When I realized he was taking his sweet time, I groaned and quickened my pace. Feeling my phone vibrate just as I entered our bedroom, I dug into my purse, still shuffling over to the bed. Lifting it out as I tossed my bag to the bed, my school was calling.

Thud!

Looking to the bed, Carter had four boxes, sitting on top of the covers. The two from the previous night, he wouldn't give me and two new ones. Cheesing super hard, I thought my face would split from me smiling so wide. *This is why he didn't wanna come up the steps with me!* I thought as I tore through the festive wrapping paper of the first box.

"What is..." I stopped talking as I pushed the sheer fabric from the box.

Tearing open the second box, I recognized the labeling. *Shoes!* I giggled as I opened the third. Gasping as I pulled a dress from the biggest box, a piece of it fell to the ground as I bent over to see it was a garter.

"Oh my God!" I laughed to myself, realizing the whole reason for our outing.

Carter was acting so impatient and weird this morning because he was on a mission. One to lure me out of the house so he can do this. Hugging the dress to my chest as I plopped down on the bed, I heard paper crinkling as I shot back up. It was a note. Smiling even more as I lifted it up, I read off Carter's instructions.

Mani we here!

You Knew this day was coming, so don't be doing all that crying and carrying out. Jump in the shower, wash off this morning, and use the Burberry shit I like. And the sesame oil you like rubbing your body down with after you get out. Get dressed and don't forget the garter Shawty. I love you!

See you at the alter, Mrs. Banks.

Carter S. Banks

P.S. Make sure you ain't got no panties on!

"Carter!" I giggled as my face flushed from the last part of his note. "I'm wearing panties!" I was talking to myself as I got undressed.

Knowing him, he'd try something nasty while removing my garter... In front of his entire family and I didn't want to give him a reason to. Fully naked, I did as I was told. Jumping in the shower, washing my body with the Burberry fragrance he loved on me. Oiling my body down with my go-to moisturizer and spritzing on my perfume before I went found a sexy lace bra and panty set I could wear underneath my dress. I wanted to shock him and this was perfect.

Sliding the garter up my left leg, I twirled around in my mirror, loving this look. Flipping my hair around, my shoulders fell once I realized I didn't know what to do with it. I mean, I could flat-iron it, but that'd take me an hour. An hour of sweating and aching arms. *I'd just have to slick it back into a parted-low bun and pray no one noticed.*

Going back into the bedroom, I carefully stepped into my dress. White with a mint tint and Swarovski crystals gleaming all over, I felt like mermaid inside it. Curving up my sides. It was form-fitting and sensual. This dress could've been worn at the Met Gala by Rihanna. I felt like a contestant for Miss Universe.

"*Uh-uh!*" I heard behind me as I turned to see my sisters, Fatima and Salimah, coming through my bedroom door.

Dressed in frilly mint and cream, I could only assume Carter made them my bridesmaids. Following behind them, in the same colored dresses, were Ebony, Yelly, and Desmond's wife, Bilan. Jumping up to hug my sisters first, Fatima was already tearing up.

"How you feelin'?" Ebony asked once she got her hug in after my sisters.

"Good—"

"You better, girl!" She cooed before pulling me back into another hug. "Carter is something else!" she gushed while looking over my dress.

And after our embrace and my side hug to Bilan, who was always closed off and polite, Yelly was last. Catching Fatima's gaze, I did the unexpected, extending my arms to welcome her into them. The least I could do, considering this was my day, and I didn't want any drama.

"Thanks for coming," I told her sincerely as she beamed, looking back at Fatima and Ebony, who were glad to see us burying the hatchet.

"You look beautiful," she told me, and I did.

Not being conceited, but this dress Carter picked out for

me accented the best parts of my body. Being petite, my boobs were an average c-cup and I didn't have the big donkey dragging in the back... Just a bubble with enough grip for my man's hands—Which he was perfectly satisfied with. Still, this mermaid ensemble had me wishing I had a seashore backdrop to pose beside. There were scales of minted blue and green sequence and shimmering Swarovski crystals I didn't even want to begin thinking what it cost. I just knew it was breathtaking.

"How are you gonna wear your hair?" Ebony asked what I'd been mulling over before they came into my bedroom.

Raising my shoulders as I looked back at my reflection in the mirror near the dresser, my ebony-colored curls flowed down my back as usual. Heavy and frazzled. I'd condition then add gel and water to keep it tamed, but that wasn't going to fly today.

"I can do it," Yelly pipped up as every eye turned towards her.

Her hair was always dope and today was no different. Silky and wavy, she parted it down the middle and feathered it like Farrah.

"I don't have anything—"

"I gotta kit in the car, hold on," she held up her finger to retrieve her phone.

"Wussup baby?" It was on speaker.

"Can you do me a favor, *Papi*?" Yelly purred as our faces curled and a few of us giggled.

"*Que puedo*?" Troy responded, shocking the rest of us except Nayelis who was giggling like a crushing schoolgirl.

"I need my hair kit out the trunk."

"Dassit?"

"Yeah—*Soy tan suertudo*—"

"Yeah, real lucky," Troy cut in as he and Yelly cackled.

"Te quiero mucho, Papi y gracias!"

"*Mmhmm,*" he hummed as everybody laughed.

Yelly ended the call after that.

"Troy speaks Spanish?" Fatima asked what I was thinking as Yelly nodded her head.

"He understands it more but we're working on it... For the kids' sake," she elaborated as I nodded, knowing their children would grow up learning it because of Yelly, so why not Troy, too.

"*Ahh*, well, he can always converse with *Joseph*, if it helps," Fatima offered as Yelly's eyes lit up.

"He speaks Spanish?" She asked my sister, who was already nodding and smiling, proudly.

"He learned from his adoptive family," she told Yelly as my face crunched with confusion.

"*Adoptive*?" Me and Salimah called out together.

"Mr. and Mrs. Vasquez," Fatima shrugged like we should've known as my eyes slowly widened.

"Rico's parents?"

"That's them!" Fatima pointed at me as Salimah smacked her lips laughing.

"They might as well adopt his ass," Salimah snorted just as her phone chirped. "Yes, Ty—Where's daddy?" She smiled at her screen as she walked up to me.

"*Titi*!" Tyler beamed the second Salimah put me in the camera.

My baby had grown up so much. Swiping the tears from under my eyes, I couldn't believe how fast she grew. A year seemed like nothing but the Tyler I used to babysit and watch Nick Jr. with had flipped the script on me. Still cute as a button with Tyrone's dimples pressing into her cheeks, I could tell she was taller and color was more pronounced. Brown like butter in the saucepan. *My roux*. She was beautiful as can be, smiling back at me.

"You're getting married?" She asked me as I nodded my head, laughing. "Congrats, I'm so happy at you!" she had the girls and Tyrone, who was listening in the background laughing.

"Thank you, baby—I can't believe you're growing up on me!"

"I'm still *titi* baby," she promised me as I pursed my lips together to keep them from trembling.

"Wussup Mani," Tyrone took the phone from Tyler.

"Hey, Ty—"

"Hey, now, don't act brand new on me, shorty," he smirked as I giggled. "Where my shorty, *OG* at?"

"*Tsk*!" Salimah smacked her lips as she snatched the phone from my face.

"Whatchu tweakin' fah, dats who you is—"

"I'm also your wife," Salimah corrected him as he chuckled, making me laugh.

"Today?"

"Ty, don't play with me."

"A'ight, relax, Charli, I'm just playin'," Tyrone laughed loudly at my sister's expense. "I'm finna bring Ty to y'all... And dis other lil shorty," he paused as I looked back at my sister, confused. "Wus yo name, sweetheart?"

"Caylin," I heard her voice, and it clicked.

"Oh, that's Carter's little cousin—On his mama's side," I explained to everybody else as heads nodded and a few shoulders rose and fell.

"Yeah cuz she white—"

"Ty!" Salimah snorted while rolling her eyes. "Just bring them babies upstairs!" She ordered before the call ended.

"Them damn Taylors," I exhaled, knowing both my sisters would take offense.

"Don't start," Fatima rolled her eyes as I giggled.

"And since when do you cuss?" Salimah flicked the back of my head as I sat down.

"Since, don't worry about it..." I quipped, rolling my eyes.

"*Bitch*, I'm not Carter!" Salimah retorted, matching my impish energy.

"Not by a *long* shot," I grinned devilishly, causing all the girls to playfully swoon.

Knock. Knock. Knock.

"*Eh*, nigga whatchu doin' up here?" I could hear Ty loudly questioning who I'd assume was Troy, behind the door as Salimah rolled her eyes to the ceiling.

"Just gettin' dis for my—Hey, baby," Troy pulled Yelly into a hug as soon as she opened the door, kissing her lips. "Here."

"Thanks, Papi—How are we on time?"

"We all dressed," Troy flicked his lapel, looking back at Tyrone who wore a minty-blue colored tux, matching the detail work in my dress and the colors of my bridesmaids.

Troy's was almost the same, except his suit was a cream color with subtle mint stitching. The vest was minty too. *Okay, Carter... I see you.*

"Okay, cool—I'ma do Amani's hair and makeup and we'll be down," Yelly told Troy as she pecked his lips again. "Where's the boys?"

"Wit my mama—"

"Okay, cool, bye Papi."

Once Yelly cleared the men out, she got to work on my hair. Plugging up her curling and flat-irons, she took out bobby pins, hairspray and a few other tools to use on me. She was like a chemist at work. Silently buzzing around me, moving my face to part my hair and analyze her progress... She never broke concentration, and that was hard to do considering how silly the rest of the girls were behaving. Still, I enjoyed the camaraderie.

"Girl, hell yeah—I almost beat her ass!" Ebony giggled with the rest of us.

"I'd beat Ty ass too—"

"Why?" I chimed in. "It wasn't Collin's fault!"

"So, what!" My little sister rolled her eyes. "These hoes is disrespectful and Ty know to check a bitch before shit get disrespectful!"

"You crazy!" Ebony cackled as she slapped fives with my sister. "But I was mad at him for not shutting her down—"

"See!" Salimah pointed at me. "Not doing nothing is worse!" Salimah was insane and Ebony was teetering down the same slope at my sister.

"Whatever—"

"Look up at the ceiling for me," Yelly instructed as I obliged.

"Oou, that cute!" Fatima gasped as she came over to where I was sitting. "You be snappin', Yelly!"

"I *knows* this!" Nayelis grinned as she placed the mascara back in her kit.

Going for a spray, she didn't warn me before she coated my face. Sneezing, Yelly giggled then apologized.

"Okay—All done!" she cheered, removing her cape from my neck. "Go look!" she urged me as the gleaming eyes before me made my stomach flutter.

"*Anything for Selenasss!*" Salimah beamed as the other girls laughed.

"That was my inspiration!" Yelly admitted as I got up from the chair.

"She does look like Selena!" Fatima chimed in.

"Iconic Grammy's up-do!" Yelly gushed. "Ya know cuz of the slick dress—Curvy and sequined." She explained to the girls. "I went with a nude-matte lip, though."

"Go look!" Fatima motioned for me to go to the mirror.

I knew Nayelis did her thing, but that still didn't stop the butterflies as I cut around the corner to my closet. I wanted a full-length mirror to see myself in. Hearing everybody following behind me, my eyes started to water as I walked up slowly to the mirror. Turning around, Yelly had her hands clasped together underneath her chin as she smiled back at me.

"I don't even know what to say—"

"Don't even mention it," she told me as I fanned my face trying not to cry.

"You look pretty, *Titi!*" Tyler was standing at my side as I looked down, smiling.

"Thank you baby—"

Knock. Knock.

We all heard knocking and turned around as Fatima and Ebony scooted out of the way. Prompting everybody near the doorway to move too. My eyes almost popped out of my head.

"What are you doing here?" I whispered as Julian emerged, holding my veil in his hand.

"Your husband called me," he answered as I threw my head back, knowing it wouldn't stop my tears.

I just didn't want a black streak running down my face as I cried.

"Mani!" I heard some of the girls calling out to me as I swiped my face, hating I'd ruined Yelly's work.

"Don't cry, *Boobie*," Fatima came to my side with a tissue.

Patting the corners of my eyes, Yelly was right behind her,

touching up my makeup. This was all too much for me. Carter had gone above and beyond and I had to tell myself I deserve this because, at the moment, I was regressing to my past pessimistic ways. *I forgive myself—I forgive myself—I forgive myself!* I chanted internally as they finished with my face.

"We'll give y'all a minute," Fatima grabbed Yelly by the hand as I nodded my head.

Waiting for them to clear out, I didn't know what to say to my daddy. It's been a month since we last spoke and it was via text message. After he told me he'd have to ease me into his life, I'd done everything to push him out of mine. Crushed was an understatement and Carter understood—Actually, knowing he reached out to Julian was more surprising to me.

"You look beautiful," he smirked as he inched closer to me. "Carter definitely has my seal of approval," he chuckled as my face remained unchanged.

Watching my daddy nervously clear his throat, he knew the small talk would have to end if he wanted me to open back up to him. No more games and no excuses.

"I'm sorry, Amani," he apologized, lifting his left hand to reveal a crown. "I—" he stopped to breathe, dropping his eyes to the floor. "There's no excuse for da way I pushed you aside," he told me what I already knew. "Especially after I went through all da trouble of seekin' you out and tellin' you who I was." Julian went on as I pursed my lips together. "I'm part of da reason you're even on dis earth and I wanna maintain a part in your life," he said hopefully, but I didn't budge. "A significant one, too," he smiled and I couldn't help the corner of my mouth curling either. "If you'll have me."

"I feel like you're asking for my hand, too," I joked as he laughed. "*But...*" My shoulders fell as I got my bearings together. "Had this been another day before today—I'd never agree to this... But I've been on a healing journey, I know wouldn't be complete without you being on it with me." I told him truthfully. "But I'm not going to play second fiddle to Jomari," I put my foot down as Julian nodded his head. "I'm your daughter too and I was here first and you owe me!" I pointed my finger in his direction as he raised his arms in surrender. "Because I didn't grow up knowing you when I should've."

"You're absolutely right," my daddy didn't disagree with me as I flashed a smile. "And I'm going to do everything I can to make up for lost time—Weekend visits, whatever you want."

"Okay... I'ma gonna hold you to it," I promised as Julian walked over to me with his arms extended.

Accepting his embrace, I was instantly lifted. It's like everything in my life was coming full-circle and I loved it. *God, that man I married!* I gushed as Julian pulled back.

"You really look beautiful," he told me again, as he placed the crown on the nearest countertop. "Just like your mama, girl —It's crazy!" he beamed as he draped the veil over my hair and face.

Looking down as the sheer lace fell past my feet, I know I was breathtaking. *That was always Carter's goal whenever we went anywhere.* He wanted me to look and feel my best.

"A crown for my princess," he placed it over the veil, on top of my head. "C'mon, Mrs. Banks," my daddy held out his arm to escort me. "Let's go give em a show!"

THE WEDDING

Carter

CHECKING MYSELF OUT IN THE MIRROR, THIS CREAM-colored tux had a nigga feeling like Bond. I could handle a gun, I had taken more than a few muhfuckas out and I helped run a slick ass operation—*I was Banks! Carter Banks!* That spy shit might just be an avenue I could see myself taking. Fixing my lapel as I lifted my chin to tie my bowtie, I couldn't believe the day was finally here. After planning behind my wife's back amongst all the crazy shit going on... I could finally give her the wedding of my mama's dreams. Nah, I'm playing—This would be Amani's day. One she could look back on fondly and never forget how much I loved her. If she didn't already know by now, the sea-green should let her know I'm minted in her life forever. *You see what I did there?* Yeah, Carter Banks knew how to tie a theme together.

"Man, c'mon!" Collin huffed as he came into my closet, creamed out like his big bro. "You still ain't ready!"

"Don't I look ready?" I threw his attitude back at him as I finished my tie.

"Yeah, now," Collin quipped as I tossed my water bottle at him.

"Mani, finished?" I asked him as he nodded his head.

She wasn't normally the two-hour dresser, but I knew with today being a special occasion... It might take my wife a little longer to get her shit together. From her hair to her makeup, I gave her ample time to do her business. *I wanted that shit right.*

"You seen her—"

"*Yesss*!" Collin stressed the S at the end as I cut my eyes at him. "With boffum," he pointed to his eyes as we both laughed.

"Man, c'mon," I pushed my little brother aside as I left out the closet.

Draping my arms over Collin's shoulder, we walked from the guest bedroom, downstairs, into the kitchen. Grabbing a couple grapes off the countertop, Troy, Desmond, Ty, Ray Ray, and Travis filed through. All uniformed in mint or cream—*My brothas were clean!*

"Dis shit nice as hell," Travis complemented my impeccable taste as I bowed my head humbly.

"Carter, please tell me you're in the kitchen!" I heard my mama's voice before I saw her.

Holding my baby girl in one arm and ushering Cairo with the other, I smiled when I saw how nice my kids looked. Dot's little dress was made to look like her mother's and my son couldn't rock nothing but cream like his father. With the mint vest and handkerchief to set it off. We all paired nicely with the bridesmaids and Mani's bouquet.

"*Yoo*!" Travis's mouth fell open as he clapped his hands together, staring down at Dot. "She really got red hair!"

"You thought I was playin'?" Tyrone nodded his head up and down as his brother.

"On everything I love, I swear, I thought you and Salimah was playin', *G*—I couldn't picture a female Carter with red hair!" He laughed as I smirked while shaking my head. "Dis shit crazy—She beautiful bruh," Travis gushed as Dot watched him. "I see you lookin' at me, shorty," he pinched her cheek as she grinned. "*Yeahhh*!" Travis cheered once he got her smiling. "*Lil Red*," he couldn't get over it.

"Hey son!" My father popped in minutes later, kissing my mama on the cheek before he came over to me, shaking up. "I'm proud of you, boy."

"Awww!" Ray Ray chimed in as my father pulled me into a hug.

"You next, Raymond," my daddy told him as he took a step back.

"*Man,* hell nah, *Unc*—I got light years ahead of me before I ever jump da broom," Ray Ray slapped the back of his hand against Collin's chest as my little brother remained quiet.

"Looks like you and ya roll dawg ain't seein' eye-to-eye," my daddy laughed as the rest of us joined him.

"*Tsk!* Dats only cuz dis nigga glued to Eb—"

"Tread lightly," Collin cut in before Ray Ray could say anything disrespectful about his girl.

"Fuck you!" he told my brother while pushing him.

"Fuck you too!" Collin returned the sentiment as the both of them laughed.

"All y'all niggas soft!" Ray Ray took his rant to all of us.

"We used to be da *Bankroll Boyz*—Fuckin' deez hoes and gettin' to dis money!"

"And we still dem niggas," I scoffed as Troy nodded his head.

"Just a little older and a helluva lot smarter," Troy chimed in as I smirked, sliding my palm to his and shaking up.

"And don't refer to my wife as a hoe," I told Ray Ray as Collin nodded his head.

"Mine either—"

"And mine too!"

Opening his mouth to rebuttal, Torin came into the kitchen with eight sheiks following him, gaining the attention of the room. Having him here, I knew he'd roll in with security but I didn't think it'd be this extreme.

"Damn, man—Don't y'all sit back?" Travis asked one of the men closest to Torin as we laughed.

"I'm used to dis shit now," Torin shrugged it off as he grabbed some fruit from the same platter I took my grapes.

"You might be but I can't take dis shit," Travis groaned as he moved his elbows around. "Gimme my six feet, bruh!"

"Excuse me!" I could hear the wedding coordinator, Michelle's chipper voice as she squeezed past six of Torin's body guards.

She had her headset and clipboard in hand, dressed in an all black dress. She'd managed to pull my vision together and I was grateful for that. "It's showtime!" she announced. "Carter and the rest of the bridal party, come this way—" She turned towards Torin, eyeing all the men around him. "I know you're the prince but if they don't mind—"

"Nah, they can go witchu," Torin nodded his head as Michelle grinned.

Watching him address them in arabic, the one closest to him and Travis responded, then led the group out of the kitchen. Not wanting to admit it, but Travis was right. The room had suddenly felt less stuffy with the exit of Torin's royal court.

"Mom, dad," Michelle pointed to my parents. "Gregory will get you to your seats—I need baby Dot, so Ebony can take her… Where is she—"

"I'm right here, Michelle," Ebony popped her head into the kitchen, smiling."

"Here's baby Dot—"

"Lil Red!" Travis yelled out.

"Yes, *little red*—Okay, guys come this way!" Michelle motioned for us to follow.

"Amani's ready?"

"Yeah—I just met up with her and her dad," she told me as we followed her to the patio doors. "I'll bring them out once we get y'all out front."

"A'ight cool," I nodded as Troy put his arm around my shoulder.

"Dis is it!" He squeezed my shoulder as I chuckled and nodded.

"Already."

My house was cleared out with all the guests seated in the backyard. Banks and Kramers to the right and Rahims, Taylors, and Munoz on the left. The moment everybody was waiting for was only minutes away. Now I ain't never been scared of the spotlight, but I could feel my nerves rising as I looked out the window. I put my love and my life on display today, in front of the people who mattered most. That meant something to me. *Dis was dat grown man shit!*

"Alright—Places, everybody!" Michelle spoke into her headset and a few moments later the music cued up. And what better way to walk down the aisle than to Mint Condition.

All that you want
All that you need
Baby, we can spend this
life so blissfully
'Cause I'm just the man for you

First to step out, Collin was behind me, then Troy, Desmond, Torin, and lastly Tyrone. Ray Ray and Travis scurried to the right for their seats, catching a scowl from my mama as I chuckled. Shaking the minister's hand as I made it to the alter, he was smiling harder than me. On account of him marrying my parents twenty-nine years ago. It must've felt like deja vu.

"You're ready this, young man?" He asked me as I nodded my head confidently.

"Oh fa sho," I told him as he chuckled.

Turning to face the audience, I winked at my mama as she dabbed her eyes, smiling back at me. This was her living the dream. And I knew after today, she'd be hounding Ebony and Collin just as she did me and Amani.

As the last man stood beside me, our song faded and Stevie Wonder's You and I played next. Clenching my fist and releasing them as Ebony came out first, I was eager to see my Shawty in that dress.

Here we are
On earth, together
It's you and I
God has made us fall
in love, it's true

Salimah was last to come out with Dot in her arms, the guests were eating it up. Cooing, Ohh-ing and aww-ing as she got closer to the alter. Like I knew Dot would, she immediately jerked towards me as I laughed and shook my head. Of course, after that, she threw a fit and my mama had to jump up to get her.

"All rise for the bride!" Gregory announced the precessional as every body out here stood to their feet.

Tyler and Caylin floated through the doors, sprinkling pedals down the aisle, followed by Cairo with his pillow and rings on display. When the kids were up front, it was really show time. Tensing up as Amani and Julian came through the patio doors. She was a dream come true. Watching her veil sway to the left as the light winds kicked underneath it, reminded me of those black and white movies my mama loved so much. She was classic... In every sense of the word.

I am glad
At least in my life
I found someone

"And who gives this woman to be married to this man?" Reverend Charles questioned Julian as he and Amani made it to the alter.

"I do," Julian grinned in my direction before turning to Amani to lift her veil.

Waiting for the grand reveal. As soon as I saw Amani's face and hair, I turned, leaning to the left so Yelly could see me. Holding up the *okay* sign as she and the rest of the audience laughed. She responded with a nod and a thumbs up as I stepped down to bring Amani up with me.

"You look beautiful," I mouthed to her as she blushed and batted her eyes.

"It's a beautiful day outside, isn't it?" Reverend Charles began. "Lovely day to witness love—"

"*Amen*!" Collin blurted out behind me, causing everybody to laugh.

Noticing Ebony's tight-lipped expression only made me laugh a little harder as Amani squeezed my hands. Looking down at her, she gave me a nervous smile as I scrunched up my face. *Chill, Mani*, I used my eyes to convey that message as her shoulders loosened and her grip on my hands eased.

Even though I knew she'd be a little anxious, the turn-out wasn't a big as I could've made it. I had family spread all over Texas that didn't get an invitation. Still, shawty would have to get used to days like this... Because she fell for a nigga like me. *And I wanted the world to know how I felt about her*.

THE RECEPTION

Amani

Shivering as the AC kicked on, Carter squeezed my hand getting my attention immediately. Gazing over my right shoulder, I couldn't stop smiling. All day long, this was my only reaction when I looked at him. Well, besides the blushing that followed. The happiness I felt inside radiated, and I knew marrying this man would be one of the best decisions I'd live to make.

"You ready?" he grinned, knowing at any minute, the DJ, at the banquet hall he rented out for the reception, would announce us and those double doors leading into the dining hall would open to our families standing, clapping and celebrating our union.

"Since day one," I told him as he smacked his lips. "Are you ready?" I tossed his question back at him.

"*Tsk!* Since day one!" he repeated as I threw my head back laughing.

"So, you can say it but I can't?" I giggled as he nodded his head. "Why?"

"Cuz, I been knew what *it* was," he told me while reaching for my chin and gripping it. "I was just waitin' on you to get wit da program—"

"Oh, hush!" I playfully rolled my eyes, but I couldn't deny his words.

Carter's always told me I was the one. And I didn't doubt it for a second... Well, I did, but he'd always be ten steps ahead of my suspicions. Leaning to my left, Carter's breath on the side of my neck was now the reason behind my shivering.

"I love you, Amani Monroe Banks," he chuckled, knowing exactly what he was doing.

Kissing the space between my ear and cheek, my right shoulder rose as I giggled from the tickling of his chin hairs. Pecking until I begged him to stop, Carter gripped my chin, turning my face toward his and kissed me properly. Using his tongue, I could feel my cheeks burning as my face got hotter. Gripping the back of his head to give me a little more leverage, I bit his bottom lip causing him to laugh.

"Quit doin' dat," he chuckled as my eyes widened.

Following my gaze, Carter's smirk grew in size as he swiped the back of his hand against his lips. Utterly embarrassing. Somehow we'd missed our cue and the doors were wide open.

"Let me say it again, for da kissin' couple in da back!" The DJ joked. "For da first time and last time, in history—Carter wrote those words," he pointed at us as I grinned up at Carter. "Mr. and Mrs. Carter Banks!"

Holding my bouquet in my left hand, I held Carter's hand with my right, which he raised in the air as we walked through the doors. Screaming and clapping and cheering with our family and friends... The noise continued until we sat down.

Eating, drinking, laughing and joking, I really enjoyed this day. Carter put me on display and for the first time in my life, loved every moment of it. Mainly because I had him by my side. Protecting and leading the way. I had the perfect husband.

"We wanna toss the bouquet!" I heard Ebony call out as I looked down the party table to see her waving me over. "C'mon!" she shouted as the rest of the girls amped her up.

Getting up from my seat with Carter's help, I grabbed my mint and cream flowers and followed behind the ladies of my bridal party to the dance floor. They were cackling and slapping fives with each other as I looked over my shoulder to see Carter leaning in his chair, winking at me. Winking back, he flashed a smiled.

"What *we* doin' right here—Da toss?" the DJ came back on the mic as I nodded my head, waving the flowers in the air. "Alright, ladies!"

Hey, baby
Aww yeah
Lemme take you to Xanadu
Where is that?
Behind the groove
Well, alright... Woo!

Going back to my teenage days in Chicago, I let the music get to me. Back when me, Salimah, and even Fatima would juke and grind, like the older girls in our neighborhood. Twirling around, popping, and dropping it to the beat as Carter jumped to his feet. Giggling, I looked to see Fatima's jaw drop as she covered her mouth. Stopping while I was ahead, I knew not to do too much more or Carter would tear this place apart.

"I TOLD Y'ALL SHE WASN'T INNOCENT!" I heard Travis yelling over the music as I cut my eyes at him.

Turning my back to my girls, I counted to three internally and tossed the bouquet over my shoulders. Laughing as I twirled to see Ebony catching my flowers. All eyes immediately shifted to Collin as he shook his head. Laughing because his brother and cousins piled on him, ruffling up his hair as they yelled in his face, wishing marriage on him and Ebony.

"Can I get a chair to the floor?" The DJ asked as one of the wedding hands obliged.

It was time for Carter to retrieve my garter. This was something I didn't want to do, but I knew I had to. Carter sauntered over to me from the bridal table and he was already grinning. Cutting my eyes up at him, he ignored me. *God, please make him behave!* I prayed just as another song cued up.

Whatever you want
It's all right with me
Cuz you got that whip appeal
So whip it on me
It's better than love
Sweet as can be

Grabbing ahold of Carter's hand, he led me to the chair in the center of the dance floor. All eyes were on me, like they'd been since the ceremony began and I could feel my nerves as he sat me down. But unlike before, what Carter was about to do was nothing close to wholesome... No matter how traditional retrieving the garter was—Carter would find a way to turn it into something sexual. Going underneath my dress was just going to give him the incentive to cop a feel and a few other things before he pulled back.

Looking up at him, he was still smiling which only made me double over, too. Pleading with my eyes wasn't going to stop him, but it was worth a try. Slowly shaking his head, I smacked my lips while rolling my eyes. *See, I knew he wouldn't listen.* Dipping down so that our eyes leveled, Carter gripped my chin before winking as I blushed and giggled.

"You better act normal," he demanded before releasing my face to drop to his knees.

Somewhat confused, I could feel my face contorting before it hit me. *Oh, God!* But it was already too late because Carter was inching my dress up with a mannish grin plastered on his face. I just hoped he didn't do some of the same stuff we did in our bedroom. I mean, I was all for the freaky deaky... But only in the privacy of our own home.

"Yo mama wanted me to letchu know she see you," the DJ interrupted Carter's grinning as he looked over his shoulder and tossed his head back laughing.

Facing forward as I smirked, I knew to keep my eyes off my sisters and my mother-in-law. Even as the room erupted in laughter, I could feel my bridesmaids burning holes through my skin.

"Hurry up!" I shook my leg to get Carter's attention as he scrunched up his face arrogantly.

"Don't rush me, woman!"

"Stop—"

"Hush!" He silence me while forcefully fluffing my dress out as you'd do a towel at the beach.

Giggling and tempted to kick him, I rolled my eyes, instead feeling him pinch my leg like he'd read my mind.

"Ow—"

"You bet not!" he threatened, and we both laughed.

Diving in soon after, it shocked me there was enough fabric for him to squeeze through. Twiddling my thumbs and bitting down on my bottom lip as his fingers slid up my ankles. He wasn't going to be satisfied until he heard me squeal. *Carter why?* I thought as I felt him grip my thigh. Close to shivering as he pressed his thumbs into the inner skin near my second lips, his touching ceased for only a moment, then I felt his breath blowing against the fabric of my panties. Giggling and shaking my head, I refused to give him the satisfaction of allowing our family and friends to see me sweat.

"Carter!" I screeched, clenching my legs together as my face burned immediately.

The crowd watching started howling as they watched me bake in embarrassment. Grabbing what felt like his shoulders, Carter scooted from underneath my dress confused.

"Stop!" I mouthed as he laughed.

"What?" He wanted to play dumb, but he and everybody here knew what he was doing under my dress. "I got it!" He waved the mint garter around as he stood to his feet.

Waiting for his boys to assimilate, I watched Carter signal to Troy with one nod. Soon after, Desmond snatched Collin up and the rest of them held him still as Carter stretched the garter between his fingers like a RubberBand. Aiming for his brother, he grinned before releasing it. Smacking Collin in his, now red, face, they howled and turned him loose.

"*Lin & EBONY—IT'S MEANT TUH BE!*" Troy and Carter started chanting, then the rest of the boys chimed in until the whole dining hall was saying it.

Forcing Ebony to stand beside Collin, they both were blushing and smiling as the room continued to swoon for them. It was cute.

"Well, it looks like we know whose next!" The DJ announced as Carter pulled me from my seat.

"Why'd y'all do him like that?" I asked as Carter shrugged it off.

"Issa Banks thang," he told me as I frowned.

"Well, I'm a Banks, now," I flashed my twenty-six carats in his face as he beamed.

"You know what–You sholl is," Carter snapped his finger like he'd just realized it as I giggled. "I almost forgot–"

"Shut up," I playfully rolled my eyes as he pecked my lips.

"Already–It's time for the couples dance... Mr. and Mrs. Carter Banks," the DJ announced as the night progressed.

The laughing and talking died down as Carter took my hand into his. Already at the center of the dance floor we were waiting on the next song as Dot's crying, picked up. Turning towards Carter's mother, I could see my baby reaching out for me and I couldn't resist.

"Yo ass bet not," Carter tried yanking my hand in the direction he wanted us to go, but I broke free, scurrying over to Chandler.

Eager to get into my arms, you would've sworn she jumped. Giggling as I kissed the top of her head, she did something she only reserved for Carter, burying her face into my bosoms while gripping at my clothes to keep our bodies close. Carrying Dot back over to Carter, his expression told me he wasn't into this.

"C'mon, daddy," I was being funny, and he knew it but he kept his frown.

Walking ahead of him, to the middle of the floor, with Dot still in arms, Carter followed behind me, dragging his feet the way Cairo would do when he had chores to do. If Carter didn't know how to do anything else, he could get everybody around him laughing. And that's exactly what was happening now.

"So, Mr. and Mrs. and lil Miss Carter Banks!" The DJ changed our title as I looked over at him smiling and Carter flipped him the finger.

"Stop it," I lightly shoved him.

Leaning down towards Dot's ear, she quickly turned her face to the other side, laughing as Carter did the same. Like a game of cat and mouse, Carter moved to the other ear and got the same reaction three more times until he grabbed the back of her head, forcing her to look at him.

"Whatchu laughin' at?" Carter smiled into Dot's face as she squealed and cooed. "Just cuz you and yo mama boo'd up and shit don't mean you gon' be da baby forever—"

"Carter!" I pulled him up to me as he laughed. "C'mon," I motioned for him to wrap his arms around us.

Obliging me, the music floated through the speakers, setting the tone. Serene, the highest level of peace. And I had it. Tranquility is hard to find when you're looking for it but once I stopped, allowing the people who loved me the most to ease my traumas and my mind—Because I had a habit of overthinking everything until it overwhelmed me... I was able to obtain this moment for life.

Bae, I can't help it
It's just high, high priced velvet
Oh, the type that you blessed with
Yeah, it's high, high priced velvet

Rocking back and forth in my husband's arms with Dot snuggled up against my breast, it was almost perfect. *I just need one more ingredient to make this sauce complete.* Breaking our embrace, I scanned over the heads watching us until my eyes fell on the missing link.

"C'mere," I waved Cairo over as he beamed, zipping past

his second cousins and other children in attendance to get on the dance floor.

Extending our small circle to welcome in my bonus son, he wrapped both arms around me and Dot as Carter laughed. Hearing the crowd erupt in laughter as Carter cut his eyes down at the kids before encasing all three of us in his arms, I felt complete. Lying my head to his chest, Carter rested his chin on top of my head and rocked us softly.

All them, wanna brag
They say, "Can I have?"
I say, "Nigga, please!"
That's my bae, yes indeed...

"Whatchu thinkin' bout?" Carter whispered into my ear as I pulled back a little to look up at him.

"Still wanna get to work on the next one?" I smirked, knowing that more children meant less alone time and more group cram sessions and family nights.

Raising his shoulders halfway, Carter ran his tongue across his lips before leaning closer to my face. Feeling his cool breath against my skin, the minty freshness would've knocked me off my feet had his arms not been wrapped around my waist.

"We can put dat off," Carter responded as I twisted my lips suspiciously. "What?"

"Don't *what* me—Seriously!" I insisted, causing the both of us to laugh.

"I'm for real!" Carter retorted, but I just couldn't believe him. "*Mani...*" Carter poked the side of my head as I giggled with his index finger. "I need you right here," he kept his finger gently pressed against my temple. "All there," he exhaled as I nodded my head understandingly. "Because what good is the body..." he bit down on his lip as his eyes undressed me, causing me to flush red. "Without the mind?"

"*Oh*!" I snickered as Carter playfully turned his nose to the air. "Is that right?"

"*Sho ya right, mama!*" Carter pecked my lips, squeezing me tighter. "I want us to be straight in all facets of life—Mind, body and soul."

"Let, that sizzle in ya spirit," I giggled as he laughed with me.

"Shut up, Mani," Carter shook his head as he leaned closer, pecking my lips. "I love you."

"*Ugh!* I knew you were gonna say it!" I stamped my foot mad that I still hadn't beat him at professing my love, first.

"You gon' always come in second place tryin' love me more than I love you..."

Melting from his words, Carter knew he was smooth. Lying my head back on his chest, Carter plopped his chin on top of my head and we danced like nobody else was here. Because in truth, nobody else mattered. Just my husband, my bonus-son, my baby girl... *And I's the Mama!*

THE END!

ABOUT THE AUTHOR

Käixo is the author of multiple urban fiction series and books. She began writing at the tender age of six and hasn't stopped since. Continuing her passion for writing, Käixo and her daughter reside in her hometown of Chicago.

CPSIA information can be obtained
at www.ICGtesting.com
Printed in the USA
LVHW041949061120
670968LV00003B/386

9 798682 575282